S0-BNC-303

Home Free

SHARON JENNINGS

Second Story Press

Library and Archives Canada Cataloguing in Publication

Jennings, Sharon
Home free / by Sharon Jennings.

(The gutsy girl series)
ISBN 978-1-897187-55-5

I. Title. II. Series: Gutsy girl series
PS8569.E563 H64 2009   jC813'.54   C2009-900730-4

Copyright © 2009 by Sharon Jennings

Edited by Doris Rawson
Designed by Melissa Kaita
Cover by Gillian Newland

Printed and bound in Canada
Third Printing 2010

Second Story Press gratefully acknowledges the support of the Ontario Arts Council and the Canada Council for the Arts for our publishing program. We acknowledge the financial support of the Government of Canada through the Book Publishing Industry Development Program.

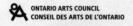

ONTARIO ARTS COUNCIL
CONSEIL DES ARTS DE L'ONTARIO

Canada Council   Conseil des Arts
for the Arts   du Canada

Published by
SECOND STORY PRESS
20 Maud Street, Suite 401
Toronto, ON M5V 2M5
www.secondstorypress.ca

For Nancy Meloshe, my redhead

Author's Note

I am in the Writing Club at school. I didn't think I'd ever get to be in the Writing Club, but I can't tell you why because that's part of my story.

Now that it's November, Miss Gowdy says it's time to write something long. A book, Miss Gowdy said. She said it can be about something that happened to us. Or we can make it up. Or we can do a little of both, which is what lots of writers do, Miss Gowdy says. They embellish the truth a little to make it better or maybe a little worse. My mother said writers tell lies. But I like the word *embellish*. It sounds like what you do with icing on a plain old white cake.

I am going to tell a story about me, and I think I'll embellish it a bit but I won't tell where. I am also going to tell some things that I'll probably get in trouble for, but Miss Gowdy says lots of writers get in trouble and it's an honorable thing. Miss Gowdy says some writers even go to jail. I hope I don't have to go to jail, but I'll probably get sent to my room.

I asked Miss Gowdy where I should start my story and she said at the beginning, but she didn't mean when I was born. She said not to confuse my story with my life.

I thought my story, not my life, started with meeting Cassandra this past summer, but then I realized it started when I first heard about Cassandra last June. So I backed it up a bit more, and I put in the part about peeing my pants by accident, even though I will probably get in trouble for telling that. But Miss Gowdy says writers have to look for patterns, and I seem to have a pattern of peeing by accident, with or without my pants on. Now I am jumping ahead, something else Miss Gowdy warned us about.

Miss Gowdy also says I should stop writing my Author's Note and just start the author part.

Chapter 1

I was two blocks from home and I knew I wasn't going to make it. I started to run, but the jiggling made it worse. I squeezed as hard as I could, but then I was walking like Frankenstein's monster. *Hur-ry hur-ry hur-ry*, I thought over and over until I was up the steps and at my front door.

It was locked.

Pee trickled down my legs. I couldn't stop it. I just couldn't squeeze anymore. I stared at my shoes and was surprised at how slowly the puddle was forming. When you squeeze really hard for so long, pee doesn't gush, I found out.

My mother opened the door. She looked at me and then

she saw the puddle and then she looked like she was eating a wormy apple.

"What on earth . . ." she said.

I toed off my runners and peeled off my socks, using only one finger, and I even took off my shorts, but not my underpants. Mom held the door open and said to go wash.

At the bathroom, I turned around. "Don't tell anyone."

"And why would I want to tell anyone an eleven-year-old girl pees her pants?"

"Please promise. Don't tell anybody."

"I promise," she said.

But when I came out of the bathroom, I heard her on the phone. I heard her say, "What a mess."

I felt something click inside me, like when the shutter closes in a camera. I got to the kitchen just as Mom hung up the phone.

"So what happened to you?" She put my lunch down in front of me.

"Mr. Morgan shooed us all out fast, and I had to go since recess. I thought I could hold it."

"Why didn't you go after recess?"

"We had the test," I reminded her. But I could tell that only reminded her about the math test we'd had the day before.

"And what about the math test?" she asked, just like I knew she would. "Did you get it back?"

I nodded.

"And?"

"And I got ninety-three."

"Ninety-three," she repeated. I knew there was more. I waited.

"Did you get the highest mark?"

I took a big bite of sandwich, just so I didn't have to answer. Just so I could keep her waiting. I swallowed and shook my head. "No."

"So who got the highest mark?"

This was really silly because my mother knew if it wasn't me then it was my future husband-to-be, David. So I lied. "Debbie," I said, and took a big gulp of milk.

"Debbie?" my mother asked. "Debbie Oldman?" The shock on her face was so funny I choked, and milk came out my nose.

Mother crossed her arms over her chest and frowned. "You're telling stories!" she said. "Debbie Oldman never gets anything but Cs. What's going on here, Lee? You pee your pants like a baby, and now you're lying."

"You lied, too," I blurted.

"I beg your pardon?" But she didn't mean she hadn't heard me. When my mother says "I beg your pardon," I know I'm in trouble.

"You told someone about me peeing. I heard you say, 'What a mess'."

"For your information, Miss Nosy, I was talking to Mrs. Fergus about something else."

"What?" I asked, not believing her. "What else is a mess?"

My mother just sniffed. My mother sniffs a lot when she's about to say something about somebody, and she thinks she's better than the somebody she's going to say something about.

Sniff.

"Mrs. Fergus is letting her cousin's daughter stay with her this coming summer."

"What's so messy about that?" I wanted to know.

"The girl's parents are dead. She's been living with someone else, and it hasn't worked out."

It took me a minute to follow all this. Then I shouted, "She's an orphan!"

"Lee! What a thing to say."

"But she is. How old is she?"

"Your age."

This was the best day of my life! Or maybe the second-best day. The best day would be when I met the orphan. An orphan my age moving in next door was beyond my wildest aspirations!

"Lee! Answer me when I speak to you."

I heard my mother, but I didn't *hear* her. "What?"

"Pardon."

"What?"

"Lee. A young lady says 'pardon'."

"Pardon?"

"I said, you didn't answer my question. Who beat you on the test?"

"David. He got ninety-eight. I came second."

"Second. He beat you by five marks."

I didn't answer.

My mother sighed. "Well, let's hope you did better on today's test."

"Today was composition. I always get the highest mark."

"Lee. You know that pride goeth before a fall."

"But it's not pride. It's the truth. I always get the highest mark on composition. And that's because when I grow up I'm going to be ..." But I saw the look in my mother's eyes. "Sorry," I mumbled.

"The highest mark for making things up. Don't go getting a swelled head about that."

She smiled as she turned away, and I knew she would brag about my marks to Mrs. Petovsky, who would then brag back about Linda's end-of-year piano recital. I had overheard them before, usually at night, when I could hide in my secret spot. They didn't know I was there in the bushes, and they said all kinds of things that I just knew I wasn't supposed to hear. They'd lean on the fence after the supper dishes were done and compare notes on the day. Mostly they talked about us kids. And the other moms, of course. (And especially so-called Mrs. Harris.)

But I am digressing, which is wrong, but Miss Gowdy says writers digress all the time, so I think that must mean I'm a writer.

"What does *digress* mean?" I asked her. (Miss Gowdy that is.)

"It means you've wandered off from your main point," she said.

So my main point right now in Chapter 1 is the orphan.

"What's the orphan's name?" I asked my mother.

Sniff. "Cassandra Jovanovich." *Sniff.*

Two sniffs! My mother really did not like all this for some reason. I wanted to find out why.

Chapter 2

I hurried back to school that day. I had to tell everyone about the orphan, Cassandra Jovanovich.

They were playing yogi.

And Kathy was with them.

It was her turn and she was at waist. She was so busy yelling at the enders that maybe she didn't see me. I backed up a foot, then another foot, then another foot, and then she turned around. I know she saw me, but it was as if she didn't see me. She just looked right through me like I wasn't there.

She turned away and said something, but I couldn't hear her. Then the others laughed and looked over at me.

Nancy waved and yelled, "Lee, come on. Take a turn."

She held up her arm and pulled on the elastic just as Kathy jumped. Which made Kathy touch. Which made Kathy furious.

"Doesn't count! Doesn't count!" she shouted.

Now I was visible. All of a sudden, Kathy could see me. She came right up to me with her fists on her hips. "What are you staring at? You did that on purpose! Made me touch!"

Then she pushed me. The others came running over. "Leave her alone, Kathy," Susan said. "She didn't do anything."

But Kathy pushed me again. I wish I could embellish this part. I wish I could tell you I pushed her back and she never bothered me again. But everyone knows what happened.

I stumbled back a bit and tripped and fell down. Kathy stood over me, staring, making fists like she was going to hit me. Then she just stopped, dropped her fists, and gave me the once-over.

"You changed your clothes. Why? Pee your pants?" Kathy laughed and everyone else laughed and I thought I did a good job laughing too, but I guess not. Kathy suddenly stopped laughing and gave a funny little smirk. (That's what my mother calls it when she doesn't like the way I'm smiling. "Wipe that smirk off your face," she says.)

"That's it! You peed your pants. You *are* a baby. I was right." Then she just turned and walked away. Linda White and Paula went with her, but Nancy and Susan helped me up.

"Don't listen to her. She's a witch."

"I hate her. She's just mean."

I watched Kathy go over and talk to other kids and point back at me.

All afternoon in class everyone made fun of me. We had spelling and whenever anyone had to spell a word with the letter P in it, they'd say P really slowly like Peeeeeeeee and look at me, and everyone else would snicker.

Except David. That's why I'm pretty sure he knows he's going to marry me one day. You can't make fun of your future bride.

But the rest of them were horrible and I knew what I wanted to do. I wanted to take my slate – of course, these are the Sixties and we don't use slates these days – and break it over someone's head, just like Anne Shirley did to Gilbert Blythe.

It wasn't fair. Kathy wasn't even in my class, but it didn't matter.

Then at recess the kids in Kathy's room said she talked about me. They were having novel discussion – they got to do *The Wind in the Willows* – and when they talked about being bossy, Kathy said there was this girl named Lee Mets who was really bossy and stupid. They said she spoke about me as if I was some stranger nobody knew. The teacher told her that was enough and to sit down, but it was too late.

The only thing that helped was thinking Kathy was just like Josie Pye who tormented Anne Shirley. And I resolved to myself that Kathy would be my affliction to bear until the end of my days.

So I didn't tell anybody about my orphan after all. The orphan would be my special friend. Tough titties for everyone else! That's what Kathy used to say – tough titties! (Don't tell my mother.)

But this is not a story about Kathy. I shall speak her name no more.

Chapter 3

Lots of kids live on my street. I usually don't play with most of them because they're heaps younger or older. But last June, when the sky stayed light forever, we all started getting together for hide-and-seek. It was fun with so many kids, but mostly I just liked being out till it finally got dark.

Sometimes I'd sneak away from the game and hide in my secret spot. It's in the corner of my backyard, between our cedar hedge and Mrs. Petovsky's bramble bushes and Mrs. Carol's fence, and there's a sort of little clearing in the middle of everything just big enough for me. I'd lie on the grass and look up through my "sky window" and see the stars and think about what our minister read from the Bible about the heavens and the earth and about dividing the light from the dark. I'd get all shivery down my back just like the time I snuck into the Sanctuary when it was all dark and there wasn't anyone there. The Sanctuary with a capital S is the part of the church you go to on Sundays to sing and pray and listen to the minister. I snuck in one time when it wasn't for church, and I felt like I was full of electricity. And I just knew I wasn't alone in there, let me tell you! It was spooky, but not scary-spooky. That's how I felt looking at the stars.

I like the word *sanctuary*. Miss Gowdy says writers have to like words and I like this one because it sounds mysterious. I asked Miss Gowdy what it means, but this time she took a deep breath and said, "Look it up in the dictionary." So I did, and it means "a holy place." In a church it's the holy place around the altar, and that makes sense because if you look at the word, it has a T exactly in the middle, looking just like a cross. Sanc t uary. Anyway, in olden days people could be protected from enemies if they could just get to the altar before being caught. From what I can figure, it was kind of like yelling "Home Free!" when you're playing hide-and-seek.

I was glad Miss Gowdy made me look up sanctuary. Now I look up lots of words all the time. If you ask a dictionary, you always get an answer. I wish adults were like dictionaries. I wish my mother would answer all the questions I have to ask. Why couldn't she just tell me about Cassandra Jovanovich without me having to ask so many questions? She always makes me feel nosy, and I'm glad a dictionary doesn't.

Cassandra Jovanovich. "Cas-san-dra," I said again, counting on my fingers. Three syllables. "Jo-van-o-vich." Four syllables. It wasn't fair. I wondered if she called herself Cassandra. Or she might be Cass or Cassie or C.J. I am only Lee Mets. Two syllables. Of course, I am really Leanna, but nobody calls me that, not even if I ask. And I asked a lot after reading *Anne of Green Gables*, and I read *Anne of Green Gables* lots. I borrowed it from the bookmobile at least once a month. Anne Shirley really wanted to be called Cordelia Fitzgerald because she thought her own name didn't have much oomph to it. I thought about calling myself L.M., just like the writer L.M. Montgomery, but it sounded stupid, like I had got to the part in the alphabet where you go elemenopee. I tried it once when the school nurse asked my name. I said, "Ell Em," and she thought I was saying "Ellen" with a stuffed-up nose.

And Cassandra Jovanovich was an orphan.

All of the best stories are about orphans. There's *Anne of Green Gables* and *Mary Lennox of the Secret Garden*. That last one isn't the real title, but it should be. Orphans always get to be *of* somewhere. I tried this out at school this year. I told Mr. Morgan that I was Leanna of Westlawn Avenue, but he said, "Don't be stupid." If I were an orphan, I'd like to be Leanna of the Castle or Leanna of Mountain Valley. I feel very sorry for Jane Eyre. She's an orphan with a name like mine and isn't *of* anything, either.

Sometimes I pretended I was an orphan and I was adopted. If my mother and father weren't my real parents then I could make up lots of stuff about who my real parents were. Even that they were still alive and rich and royal and would come to get me one day when it was safe. Like the Little Princess who turned out not to be an orphan. This is what I did at night when my parents (so-called) wouldn't let me read in bed and made me turn out the light. I made up stories about my real parents.

I hoped Cassandra Jovanovich would be like book orphans. I hoped she'd have lots of imagination. Maybe she'd even be a writer, like me. Maybe we could write books together and become each other's *muse*. That's another word Miss Gowdy told us. It's some sort of spirit that whispers good ideas in your ear.

I hoped we could be best friends because after Kathy did you-know-what, I didn't have a best friend anymore. But more than that, I hoped we could be kindred spirits. That's what Anne Shirley called some people, the people she just felt an instant connection to, as if there was some electricity between them. Once Anne Shirley called her best friend her bosom friend, but I wouldn't want to do that. My mother won't let me say the word bosom and I don't want to get Cassandra Jovanovich and me in trouble.

I didn't have any kindred spirits my own age. I knew Miss Gowdy was one as soon as I met her, and I knew Mrs. McMillan, who teaches Sunday School, was a kindred spirit, too. But I wanted a kindred spirit who was a friend I could play with. I once had high hopes for Kathy, but that didn't work out.

I looked up the word *kindred* in the dictionary. At first, I was disappointed. It just meant "family" or "having the same blood." I have lots of family that I don't want to be kindred spirits with, let me tell you! But I kept reading down the definition and it said kindred was the same as the word *congenial*. So I looked up congenial and it means, "being the same in spirit." So I guess what I was looking for were spirits to be spirits with. Sometimes the dictionary is confusing.

I was still looking at the stars when my mother started calling for me to come in and I had to leave my secret place. Only from then on I called it my Sanctuary.

Chapter 4

The next day, I told Miss Gowdy all about Cassandra Jovanovich.

"And she's an orphan, just like Anne Shirley and Jane Eyre and she's going to be my best friend, I just know it!" I said.

Miss Gowdy smiled at me and said, "Sit down Leanna." (Miss Gowdy always called me Leanna after I asked her to.) Then she leaned forward and said, "You will have to be especially kind to Cassandra. And thoughtful."

"I am always full of thoughts," I said.

Miss Gowdy put her hand over her mouth, but I could see the smile behind it. I don't mind it when Miss Gowdy smiles at me. (Sorry Miss Gowdy, because I know you're reading this.) Because you, I mean *she*, isn't laughing at me the way most adults do.

"You certainly are full of thoughts," she agreed. "So what I should have said was you'll have to be considerate. Being an orphan in real life might not be quite as . . . as romantic as it is in books."

Miss Gowdy is still quite new at our school. She is the librarian because Mrs. Humprey was old and quit. Miss Gowdy is young and pretty and smells like lily of the valley. She is just like Anne Shirley's Miss Muriel Stacy, the new teacher who was so much nicer than the old grumpy teacher. Mrs. Humprey was always kind of rumpled-up looking and smelled like the humbug mints my Uncle Bill gives me sometimes. I pretend to eat them, but I don't because they always have lint on them from being loose in his pocket.

I don't like my Uncle Bill. He always tries to give me a charley horse on my leg. He pushes my skirt out of the way and grabs my thigh high up and squeezes, and then he laughs – but I don't. A charley horse hurts. And I don't think Uncle Bill should go near my underpants. One day in kindergarten, I showed everyone my new underpants. They were really pretty, white and lacy with colored balloons on them. Miss Swora got mad at me. She said I did a bad thing. She said it was inappropriate. I looked up the word *inappropriate* in the dictionary. Not when I was in kindergarten, but just this year. It means "not proper, not the right thing to do." So the last time Uncle Bill tried to give me a charley horse up near my underpants, I told him it was inappropriate and smacked his hand. Everyone laughed at me. I thought that was inappropriate of everyone, and I stood up and said so. I got sent to my room. I don't know why.

Anyway, everyone likes Miss Gowdy, even the boys, and especially David. She reads to us every time our class has library day, and she says she reads books that we might not be able to read ourselves. She wants to stretch our minds, she says. The first book she read was called *The Pearl* and it was wonderful and sad and made me feel hurt inside when I listened. I wish I could write like that.

One day I told Kathy I wanted to be a writer.

"I'm going to be a model," she said. Then she talked all about what models do and who her favorite model is, and we didn't talk about me at all.

Kathy could be a model. She could be a model for *Seventeen* magazine. She is the most beautiful girl in our grade. Or even in our whole school. And I don't mind saying so because I am a writer and writers want to get at the truth, Miss Gowdy says. (My mother always says, "Tell the truth and shame the devil," but I don't know what that means.) So even though Kathy makes fun of me all the time, and isn't a friend at all, I will tell the truth. She's taller than anyone, even the boys, and she has brown hair that curls and big brown eyes and a small nose and, well, she just is pretty. All the boys think so, too. And she already wears a brassiere. She laughs at all the rest of us girls because we still wear undershirts.

"Kathy wears a brassiere," I told my mother one day. "Can I have one?"

My mother went all red. "Don't be silly," she said.

I persevered. "But why? Why is it silly? Why can't I have a brassiere?"

"That's enough, Lee."

And that was it. *Perseverance* means "to continue on despite difficulties," but when my mother says "That's enough," she means it. My mother refused to talk about it anymore. But maybe I didn't really mind because the boys pull on Kathy's brassiere strap and call it an over-the-shoulder boulder-holder. Kathy just laughs, but I think I'd die.

I think I just digressed. (And from now on, I won't talk about you-know-who anymore.)

Miss Gowdy started a Writing Club last year when I was in grade five because lots of us wanted to write books like the ones she reads to us. The club met twice a week after school on Tuesdays and Thursdays for one hour. And David was in it. I could be with David two hours a week talking about books in earnest, and not just the way we do in class with people who don't care. (*Earnest* means "seriously zealous" and *zealous* means "passionate ardor" and *ardor* means "heat in the affections" and so it all works out because I have seriously zealous ardor about David and books.)

But my mother wouldn't let me join the Writing Club. She said reading fairy tales was a waste of time and writing them was even worse. She called all books fairy tales, even when they weren't about fairies. If they were made-up stories like *Anne of Green Gables* she called them fairy tales. She said I should just read my Bible instead. Or the *Presbyterian Register*, which is all about good religious Presbyterians doing good works, like going far away to be missionaries. My father said I always have my nose in a book. This is true because if I'm not wearing my glasses, I have to have my nose in the book to see. But that isn't what he meant. He always said "your nose in a book" as if I was doing something wrong. I don't know why.

I told my mother I wanted to be a writer, but she wanted me to be a teacher or a nurse. "That's what good girls do," she said.

"What do bad girls do?" I asked.

"That's enough, Lee."

"Why?"

"Mind your manners, Lee."

"But I want to know. Why is it enough? What do bad girls do?"

"Do you want to go to your room? That's what happens to bad girls."

"No."

"That's better. Then, after you work for a year or two, you can get married," my mother said.

"But I don't like anybody," I said. (This was a lie because I am going to marry David, but I don't want my mother to know.)

One day I tried something different.

"I want to be a *famous* writer when I grow up," I explained. "I'll be a *millionaire!*"

"And just who do you think you are?" she asked.

This stumped me. I had a pretty good idea of who I was, but from her tone of voice I didn't think she meant Leanna Mets of Westlawn Avenue.

"Miss Gowdy says I'm a good writer. Miss Gowdy says that I –"

"Oh, 'Miss Gowdy says.' And what makes Miss Gowdy so smart?"

But I knew the answer to that one.

"She's a teacher!" I exclaimed. "She's a good girl! So there!"

I got sent to my room. And while I was sitting in my room, something occurred to me. When my mother asked who I thought I was, maybe she was hinting that I was really adopted! Maybe I *was* an orphan and didn't know it!

I made up a really good story that night, let me tell you!

Chapter 5

Cassandra Jovanovich moved here in July. Everybody knew she was coming, even though I didn't breathe a word to anyone – cross my heart and hope to die – and lots of girls showed up on her porch the night she came. Even Kathy. Everyone wanted to see what an orphan looked like up close and everyone was hoping that if she was any good she'd end up liking them best. (I thought I would just die if she ended up liking Kathy best because I needed a new best friend to replace Kathy, who didn't work out so good, as I said before. And Kathy was probably there just to spite me.)

So on this most important night of my life, I was baby-sitting Mrs. Carol's baby. For ten cents I had to take her for a walk in her buggy to get her to sleep. But she kept crying, so I picked her up and she let out a big burp and stuff came out all over my shoulder.

All the girls saw it. I don't know how a tiny baby can burp so loud but she did, and everyone turned to look from way up there on the porch, and they all saw what happened.

Including Cassandra Jovanovich!

She had red hair!

An orphan with red hair moved in beside me and I was so mortified I'd never be able to talk to her ever! I looked up the word *mortified* in the dictionary and it means "to be ashamed," but it comes from really old words meaning "to make dead." I wanted to make dead right there on the sidewalk, let me tell you! It was the most tragical disappointment of my life! That's what Anne Shirley said when she thought Diana might not like her.

I shoved Mrs. Carol's baby back in the carriage. That's the truth. I shoved her and I hope I don't go to jail. Of course, I've seen Mrs. Butterfield shove her kids lots of times and she isn't in jail and I think she should be. I ran up the street pushing the carriage. I thought about just going and going and running away from home, but then I'd really have to go to jail. If I took Mrs. Carol's baby with me, or if I just left Mrs. Carol's baby on the side of the road. Either way, I'd go to jail.

So I walked around the block and snuck into Mrs. Carol's house from the other way and gave them back their baby. Then I snuck in my back door to change my shirt. Then I wondered how I could live the rest of my life never going outside again. I decided I'd better make a trip to the bookmobile and get lots of books to read before I became a hermit.

But before I left, I snuck a peek at Mrs. Fergus's porch. Cassandra Jovanovich was there all by herself. Maybe the other girls all had to go home. Maybe they didn't like the orphan up close. Cassandra looked very orphan-like, sitting there all alone, with her red hair hanging over her face, and suddenly I thought maybe baby burp-up wasn't so bad. I walked over to Mrs. Fergus's.

"Where did everybody go?" I asked her.

"I told them to go away."

"Don't you want friends?"

"Not nosy ones."

I wondered if she meant me, too, because I had just asked two questions. I waited, but she didn't tell me to go away.

"My name is Lee."

Then I made a face, the one I make when my mother says to be careful my face doesn't freeze like that. "I meant to say my name is Leanna, but nobody calls me that so I keep forgetting myself."

"I'll call you Leanna if you call me Cassandra."

"Isn't Cassandra your name?"

"Yes, but I get Cass all the time. The people I was with two before this said that Cassandra was too fancy a name for me."

"Just like Anne Shirley!"

"Who's that?"

"You know, Anne of Green Gables. She wanted to be Cordelia Fitzgerald and everybody laughed at her."

Cassandra didn't know what I was talking about. "You're an orphan," I explained to her. "There are lots of books about orphans. You have to read them. Especially *Anne of Green Gables*. It's the best."

I had high hopes Cassandra would look tremendously excited and ask to read the book right now, this very minute, so that we could start being best friends immediately.

"That girl Kathy doesn't like you," Cassandra said.

I think I must have looked very stupid.

"She told you that? Already?"

Cassandra nodded. "She says you're a little . . . you know . . ." She put her finger up to her head and twirled it around. ". . . Nuts. She says you talk about orphans all the time and I should watch out. She said she felt sorry for me living next door to you."

Kathy! I hated her! She'd already ruined Cassandra for

me! I knew I was going to cry. I stood up. I had to go home. I had to get away and be by myself. I started down the steps.

"Aren't you going to ask me why I'm an orphan?"

I stopped. Of course, I wanted to ask.

"All the others wanted to know. They wanted to know how my mother and father died."

In my heart of hearts I wanted to know, too. But she pushed her hair off her face for a second and I could see her eyes get sort of squinty and I suddenly knew if I asked, she'd send me away.

Then I got really considerate all of a sudden. I thought about being an orphan myself and always having to answer questions. So I just said, "Do you want to tell me why you're an orphan?"

Cassandra shoved her hair back over her face.

"Maybe."

So I waited but she didn't say anything more, so I figured that maybe her maybe meant some day, but not now. Then I got tired of saying nothing.

"Do you want to come to the bookmobile with me?" Even though it didn't look like I'd have to be a hermit, I still needed some books. Because right now, it didn't look like I'd have anyone to play with this whole summer.

I looked up *hermit* in the dictionary. It means "someone

who lives in seclusion." And *seclusion* means "to shut yourself off from others." Cassandra Jovanovich was doing a pretty good job of that. But maybe she was like me. I didn't really want to be a hermit. Sometimes, I just wanted to be alone.

Chapter 6

Cassandra went inside to ask Mrs. Fergus if she could go to the library with me. And when she came out, she was wearing go-go boots and a John Lennon hat pulled down low over her eyes. I wanted go-go boots for Christmas last year, but my mother said no. She said white boots were ridiculous. And I couldn't get a John Lennon hat because my mother doesn't like The Beatles. I felt just like Anne Shirley wanting a dress with puffed sleeves. I even said the same thing to my mother that Anne said to Marilla.

"Oh, but Mother," I said, "it would give me such a thrill to have go-go boots or a John Lennon hat."

And my mother said the same thing back to me that Marilla said to Anne.

Sniff. "You will have to do without your thrill." *Sniff.*

My favorite Beatle is Ringo or sometimes George. Everybody else loves Paul or John, so I thought I should be considerate and show ardor to the other two. I have one Beatles record. I bought it with my babysitting money, but I only play it when my parents are out. They say it isn't music. That's just silly because I dance to it, so it must be music. After The Beatles were on TV on *The Ed Sullivan Show*, some of us decided to put on a Beatles show at school. We wore pants and we got white shirts and ties from our dads and we wore our hair combed over our eyes. Then we put on the record and pretended to sing. I looked at David the whole time we sang "I Want to Hold Your Hand."

Way back then I thought he liked me as much as I liked him. He gave me a Valentine and on it he wrote a Beatles song except he changed the words. David wrote: "She was just nine-ein, and she didn't look fine-ein, 'cause the way she looked was way beyond repair, oh she'll never dance with another, because she was smothered by her mother," so I thought maybe he loved me. I also thought *I'm a better writer than he is and that's why I always get the highest mark on composition.*

"You look so . . . (I wanted to say groovy, but Kathy says I'm not cool enough to say groovy) . . . so neat."

"Try it on." Cassandra gave me her John Lennon hat. Then she frowned. "It doesn't look so good on you."

"It's my glasses. And my ponytail." I took off my glasses and pulled out my hair. I pulled my hair over my eyes and down my face like Cassandra. "How's that?" I asked.

Cassandra nodded. "You should get one."

"My mom won't let me. And besides, without my glasses, I can't see."

On our way to the bookmobile, I showed Cassandra where everybody lived.

First I pointed out where four of the Debbies live.

"Can you believe it? We have six Debbies on our street. Most of them are nice, but you have to watch out for Debbie Oldman. She cries whenever she loses games and tells her mother on us and then her mother comes out and calls us brats and says she's going to phone our mothers. My mother says Mrs. Oldman thinks she's special because her sister's husband's brother is a mayor somewhere. Then my mother sniffs. My mother doesn't like people who think they're special. I don't know why. I want to be special when I grow up. Don't you?"

Cassandra looked down at the sidewalk. "I guess so," she said. "I'm sure not special right now."

I remembered to be considerate. "Yes you are. You've got red hair and I'd die for those boots!"

I showed her where the twins Ronnie and Donnie live.

"They're a grade younger than me and they like to beat people up. I stay out of their way but there are some kids who will pay Ronnie and Donnie a dime to beat someone up for them. One time Donnie pushed me down and pulled my hair because Paula asked him to. He said it would have been worse, but Paula only had a nickel."

I explained that Paula is fat and picks her nose and lives in the corner house. Nobody likes her because she's a show-off and smells like dirty underwear.

I showed Cassandra where Nancy lives. Her father drives a taxi and sometimes, if it's raining, he'll load all the kids he can fit into his cab. So you have to know where Nancy lives because if it's raining, you have to get there early enough to get a ride to school.

"Once I got there first, and I never did that again because I got stuck with Paula sitting on my lap. She caught me making a face and the next day is when Donnie half beat me up."

Then I pointed across the street. "The house with the big tree is where Susan lives. I either play with her a lot, or I don't play with her at all. Her mother doesn't like me, I can tell."

"How can you tell?" Cassandra asked.

"Well, sometimes when Susan asks me to stay for lunch

or for dinner or for breakfast Mrs. Tupper says in a very loud voice, 'Doesn't Lee have a home of her own? Tell her to eat there,' like I can't hear. I hate it when adults say things loud enough on purpose for me to hear."

Cassandra rolled her eyes. "Adults always say stuff like that in front of me. I'm an orphan. I don't count."

"How inconsiderate," I said. And I added, "And how inappropriate, too! When I have children I won't say mean things. And get this. I hate margarine and Mrs. Tupper uses margarine, the kind in the bag with the red blob of color inside, and you have to squish it all around to make the margarine yellow. My mother says it costs less and Mrs. Tupper is cheap."

The biggest house is where Linda White lives. She is an only child. She wasn't supposed to be an only child, but from what I have overheard from my Sanctuary, something is wrong with Mrs. White. My mother and Mrs. Fergus and Mrs. Carol and Mrs. Petovsky all talk about Mrs. White and my mother sniffs and everybody else raises their eyebrows a lot.

So I told Cassandra, "I don't know why they don't like Mrs. White, but I know why they don't like Linda. She always wants to play doctor. She's always trying to get us to take our clothes off so the doctor can look at our bums. My mother caught us once and dragged me home and smacked my beee-hind with a hairbrush. She always calls it my beee-hind when she's mad enough to spank me. She said we were dirty and filthy and we'd end up like so-called Mrs. Harris."

I showed Cassandra where Mrs. Butterfield lives.

"She hits her kids all the time, but not like my mother wallops my beee-hind. None of her kids are old enough for me to play with so none of them are my friends, but I feel sorry for all of them. Sometimes they come to school with black eyes or bruises on their arms and they say they fell down the stairs. How can three kids fall down the stairs so many times all the time? My mother says it is none of my business. My mother also tells me to keep my hands to myself. One day I saw Mrs. Butterfield smack Laura across the mouth. I saw Laura's eyes go all dark like the black part was running into the colored part and I heard Mrs. Butterfield say, 'That'll learn ya.' I don't know what Laura has to learn, but Mrs. Butterfield should learn to keep her hands to herself, even if it isn't any of my business. The next day at school Laura was missing a tooth, and I gave her the dime I got from the tooth fairy for the tooth I lost that week. After I wondered if I should have given my dime to Donnie and Ronnie to beat up Mrs. Butterfield."

Cassandra Jovanovich had been walking slower and slower and I had to stop and wait for her to catch up. She had her arms crossed over her chest and she was glaring at me. "Do you ever stop talking?" she demanded. "Maybe I don't care if some old witch hits her kids. I don't even know them."

Well! I turned away and kept walking. She could follow me or not.

And in a minute she tugged at my arm. "I'm sorry," she mumbled behind her hair. "I just don't like hearing about stuff like . . . like that. About hitting."

I linked arms with her. "I know," I said. "I mean, I don't know that you don't like it. I mean, I don't like it either. And Mrs. Butterfield *is* a witch, you're right. My mother smacks me sometimes, but not like Mrs. Butterfield. She hits."

Cassandra nodded.

The hardest I ever got smacked was when I said a dirty word. I didn't know it was a dirty word and I didn't know I was going to say it. I just opened my mouth and the dirty word came out. I didn't plan on it. And I didn't know what it meant. Sometimes boys write it on fences, so maybe it just got lodged in my brain. My mother screamed and lurched toward me and chased me around the living room and the dining room and down the hall and into my bedroom. Then we went around the bed a few times before she caught me and took the hairbrush to my beee-hind. I sure wish

I knew what that word meant. I guess I could have asked my father. When he came into my bedroom that night, he asked what I had said. I wouldn't tell him. What if he got mad and chased me around the bed a couple more rounds? He said he'd heard all about it from my mom. Of course, my mother never says bad words, so she wouldn't tell him what bad word I'd said. He kept asking and asking. Finally he said goodnight and told me not to worry. Mom would be fine in the morning. Well, that's great. What about my beee-hind? Would it be fine in the morning? And then, as I was drifting off to sleep, I suddenly knew why my dad wanted to know. He probably wondered if it was one of the bad words he says all the time. I figured out that he was probably in trouble with my mother, too.

"That's Kathy's house." I pointed to the house with the blue door.

We walked along for a couple more houses.

"Well?" asked Cassandra Jovanovich.

"Well what?"

"Aren't you going to go on and on and tell me everything there is to know about Kathy? About what her mom says to you and if they eat margarine?"

I got it. "You're making fun of me for talking so much." I turned and stared at Kathy's house. Then I kept walking.

"I forgot. She hates you, right?"

I kept walking.

"Why does she hate you?"

"Now who wants to ask questions?"

We glared at each other. Cassandra looked away first. "I'm sorry."

She looked so sad. Suddenly I blurted, "We were best friends. Now she hates me. That's all." I wasn't going to say anything else, but the words came out. "Her dad is creepy. He has a collection of beer mugs and the handles are bare-naked ladies."

"Ewww."

"He used to give us Orange Crush in them and tell us we were drinking beer."

"And you had to hold the handles?"

I nodded.

"Ewww."

Then I remembered my vow. "I don't want to talk about her," I said. "From now on my lips are sealed."

By then we were at another Debbie's house, Debbie Walker.

"She has four brothers and sisters and a huge big boxer dog they call Tinkerbell, and I like her mother best. She makes Jell-O Popsicles and chocolate chip cookies almost every day and lets me eat as much as I want. And she lets me put sugar on grapefruit if I'm there for breakfast. Her kids also put sugar on tomatoes, but I think that's just plain silly. Her house is always messy and smells like five kids have peed somewhere, not just in the toilet, and she never yells at me and she tells my mother I am very polite. My mother just sniffs. Her name, Debbie's mother's name, is Muriel. I think I will name one of my children Muriel. I am going to have five children. Which reminds me. Do you have brothers or sisters or are you an only orphan?"

"Muriel is a nice name. Old-fashioned."

I had done it. Asked a question she wasn't going to answer. So I started talking again. "For a long time I didn't know what my mother's name was. I mean, I knew people called her Marjorie but one day I suddenly realized that she had a name like I did, and she wasn't just Mother. So I asked her, 'Is Marjorie your name?' And she said 'None of your business.' Why is it none of my business? Why are so many things none of my business? My mother says 'None of your business' all the time. When I grow up I want to know why."

"Rita," said Cassandra Jovanovich.

"What?"

"My mother's name is Rita."

She said it in such a strange way, like . . . like the name was something bad in her mouth and she had to spit it out. And I knew I couldn't ask her why.

"That's a nice name," I told her. I tried to make myself look all sorrowful and deeply understanding and considerate and thoughtful. "It sounds Spanish."

"I hate it."

Well, of course, I wanted to ask a question.

Good thing we were at the bookmobile.

Chapter 7

A bookmobile is a truck with books. A big truck, like you'd put your furniture in if you were moving. It goes around to places that don't have a library built of bricks that stays put in one spot.

Every Wednesday the bookmobile comes to the plaza near us. It has two doors, and you line up to get in one door and you leave by the other door. Only so many people can get in at one time because inside, the sides of the truck are lined with books, floor to ceiling. You make your choices and you give your card to the librarian at the other door. She writes down when your book is due back and if you're late, you pay five cents. I am never late because I read all my books fast and I'm always waiting for next Wednesday.

Miss Gowdy told us that we are very lucky. She told us that in some places in Africa the library is a camel that goes to the people who move about the desert. And in Lapland, the children have to take books out for six months because they're with the reindeer for that long. That would leave me with five months, three weeks, and four days with nothing to read.

I like the bookmobile. It smells like books. I've been to the stay-put kind of library but they don't smell the same. I figure they're too big and have too much space in them and then you can smell the people more than the books. And not everyone smells as nice as Miss Gowdy, let me tell you!

I showed Cassandra where the children's books are and I told the librarian that Cassandra Jovanovich was new. So the librarian gave her a form to fill out and I saw Cassandra go all red when she looked at it. She pushed her hair over her face and then she crumpled the form up and ran outside. But she didn't know the rules so she ran out the door you come in and people yelled at her.

I didn't know what to do. I wanted to run after her, but I wanted to get books, too. But with Cassandra gone, people were looking at me. I hurried down the truck and out the proper door.

Cassandra was sitting on a bench near the fountain.

"I hate filling in forms. They always ask about my parents. And where I live. I hate it."

I hadn't thought about this. Book orphans never seem to mind that they're orphans.

"I've lived in so many different houses I can't remember them all. I can't remember the names of all the schools I've gone to. Sometimes I can't remember the names of the relatives I've stayed with."

I hadn't thought about this either. Then I realized that Cassandra's life up to now was like Anne Shirley's life before she went to Green Gables. She was always being passed around to lots of people who made her do lots of chores.

"Why don't you ever stay?" I asked.

"They don't want me. Sometimes I don't want them. One time I wanted to stay. Philip and Cathy were nice. They were going to let me take drama lessons."

"So why did you leave?"

"They got their own baby."

"But you could have helped with the new baby. Anne Shirley always helped with people's babies," I explained.

"I wanted to. I said I would help, but Cathy said both of us were just too much. She said it wouldn't be fair to me. So I went to someone else. But before I went she bought me the John Lennon hat and go-go boots."

"She felt sorry for you," I said.

"She felt guilty's more like it," answered Cassandra.

"And then you came here?"

"No. When I left Cathy's I went . . . I went somewhere else. I hated it."

Cassandra pushed her hair back off her face for a second and I could see her eyes start to go black like Laura's when Mrs. Butterfield hit her. I didn't know what to do so I said, "Wait a minute," and ran to the store, but the grocery store, not Sid's Variety Shop, and I used my nickel to buy us a banana Popsicle. I split it on a brick, and I was happy it cracked fairsy right down the middle. We walked home, not talking, just trying to lick the drips before they dripped down our arms and made our elbows sticky.

I asked Cassandra to play tomorrow and then I snuck away to my Sanctuary. But nothing shivery happened that night. I kept seeing how Cassandra's eyes had gone all black and I felt heavy inside. Cassandra didn't know anything about Anne Shirley, but I was pretty sure she knew all about Anne's depths of despair.

Chapter 8

The next day I called on Cassandra Jovanovich really early. Mrs. Fergus told me to go home and come back later. They were eating breakfast. I would have eaten some of their breakfast if they'd asked me.

I went into my backyard to the tree by the corner, where I can see into Mrs. Fergus's kitchen if I climb to the first branch. We didn't always have this tree and I sure couldn't climb it when we first got it. We had just moved into our new house – and it was a new house, nobody had ever lived in it before, not like the old house we'd just left – and the backyard was just a lot of mud. My dad said we needed some trees and he knew just the place to get them. I thought we'd be going to the nursery like we did for the flowers in the front, but my dad said he had a better idea. He didn't tell me what and by dinnertime I thought he'd forgotten, but then, when it was dark he said "Let's go." (I hope I don't have to go to jail for this next part. It happened a long time ago so maybe nobody cares now.)

My dad and I got in the Rambler, but my mother stayed home. Then we drove around the corner to the new school. My dad parked the car and we got out and went into the field. The field isn't there anymore because lots more new houses got built. But back then it was there and there were lots of trees in it. Saplings, my dad called them. And right away he started digging, and pretty soon we carried five saplings back to the car. My dad tied down the trunk like we had a Christmas tree in it, and we drove home.

My mother just sniffed when she saw us.

"Aren't you breaking the law?" she asked.

"It's a field, Marjorie. We didn't steal from anyone," my dad said.

"Then why did you wait until it got dark?"

My dad winked at me. "Didn't want anyone else to steal my good idea. Let everyone go to the nursery and pay."

Sniff.

"And besides," said my dad, "they're poplars. Poplars are weed trees. You can't steal a weed."

And the next day, my dad and I planted five weed

saplings along one side of our yard. "Just you wait," my dad said. "One day these will be great big trees. Lots of shade. Lots of privacy from nosy neighbors."

It was hard to believe him because the saplings looked so scrawny. But he was right. Weed trees grow really fast. And soon, well, in three years, we had four (one died) really nice trees. And now I can climb them and sit under them and use them to put on plays (that's another chapter). And I feel just like Anne Shirley who named her trees and talked to them and imagined all sorts of stories about them.

We have a really thick hedge on the other side of our yard, but my dad didn't steal those cedars. He went out and bought them and he bought such really big ones that the nursery delivered them to our house. That's because my dad really wanted privacy from the neighbors on that side. Not the neighbors we have now. Not the Carols and their baby. They're nice people. But the neighbors before them were not nice. Not to me, anyway. They had a little girl named Susan who was a grade behind me. Susan didn't play with me much to begin with. Her mother didn't like me. She said I was forward. I looked up *forward* in the dictionary and the nearest I could get to what Susan's mother meant was that I was bold or presumptuous. So then I had to look up *presumptuous* and it meant "disrespectful behavior." Well!

I didn't think I was presumptuous at all, but I like the word. It feels meaty. I decided to start using it myself.

I didn't care too much that I couldn't play with Susan. She was dippy. She only played with her dolls and she wasn't allowed to play games if she might get dirty. I don't know why she couldn't get dirty because every day at four o'clock she had to go inside to get washed for her daddy. That's what she called him. So did her mother. My mother calls my father your father or Earl. That's my dad's name. Earl. Anyway, Susan's daddy came home at five o'clock every day and Susan had to be fresh out of the tub. And if I was playing at her house, her mother always sent me home. "Run along, Leanna. Susan's daddy will be home momentarily."

My dad gets home at five o'clock every day, too, but I don't have to wash for him. I have to wash my hands for dinner, but that's all. And I always have a bath Saturday night to be ready for church, and I wash my face every morning, so I don't know why Susan's grandmother called me a dirty little girl. I think she's inappropriate *and* presumptuous.

But one day, my dad brought home a swing set for our backyard. It was bright red with two swings and a slide. And suddenly, Susan was allowed to play with me a lot more. At my house. Until I hit her. But it was an accident. She was so dippy that she stood right behind the swing. And I swung back and the metal seat hit her near her eye.

She fell over and screamed and I jumped off the swing and before I knew what to do, her grandmother was in our backyard. She picked up Susan and said I was a horrible child, and they got Susan off to the hospital right away. She was pretty much okay, but she had to wear a patch over her eye for a few days. I wasn't allowed to see her. When I went over to her house the next day, they sent me home and told me I couldn't play with Susan ever again. They said I wasn't suitable.

Susan and her mother and grandmother and daddy moved a few months later. My mother sniffed and said, "Good riddance." Which reminds me. I didn't get sent to my room when I hit Susan by accident. Susan's parents came over and told my parents that I was an *"en-fun terreee-bluh"* and what were they going to do about it? My mother got that wormy-apple-in-the-mouth look. She just looked at my father and said, "Earl?" and then she went inside our house. My father asked Susan's parents to get off our property and then he went inside. (I know because I just happened to be reading my book near the front window.)

And then the next day, my father went to the nursery. And the day after that, a big truck came and a huge cedar hedge went up.

Chapter 9

Anyway, I sat in the tree branch that was the best for spying and as soon as I saw Mrs. Fergus at the sink doing the breakfast dishes, I went and called on Cassandra Jovanovich again. I had something to ask her.

"Do you have a best friend?"

"No."

"Why not?"

"I'm never anywhere long enough."

But I had already figured this out. I explained it to her. "I don't think you have to know somebody a long time to be best friends. I think sometimes you just know. I think it's like the princess who falls in love with the prince at first sight in fairy tales. I liked you right away and I think we should be best friends."

Cassandra shoved her hair out of her face.

"Why? Why do you like me so much? You don't know anything about me. You like me because I'm an orphan and I have red hair like your stupid Anne Shirley." Then she shoved her hair back over her eyes.

Well! This was not what I would put in a book if I were writing it. That's what I like about writing. Anything can happen just the way I want if I'm the writer. But in real life, people say things I don't like. Of course, I could have embellished this part, but I didn't. I could have embellished it so it was more like when Anne Shirley met Diana Barry. They spoke very fancy language, and said "Wilt thou be my bosom friend?" and "I love thee, o faithful friend of my heart," and stuff like that. But maybe Cassandra Jovanovich will read this some day, and so I couldn't embellish.

So I said, "I want to like you. I wanted to like you as soon as I heard about you. I like reading about orphans. I couldn't believe I was going to get an orphan for a next-door neighbor."

Then she went all red and yelled. "What is so special about being an orphan?"

So I yelled back. "Well I want to be an orphan, so there!" I couldn't believe I said it, and I clapped my hand over my mouth.

She got that look like she wanted to spit something out. Then she said, "Kathy was right. You are cuckoo."

Kathy!

"You only like me because I'm an orphan? Well thanks a lot! And you want to be an orphan so we can start a stupid club or something?"

Then she jumped up and ran out of the room. I heard a door slam. I heard something being thrown.

Mrs. Fergus came running up from the basement. "What happened? What did you do, Lee?"

"Nothing. I didn't do noth . . . anything."

Mrs. Fergus just glared at me. "Well something has upset Cassie. I think you'd better go home."

So I went home.

Chapter 10

I went straight to my bedroom and slammed my door. (Of course I only did this because I knew my mother was at the store. Otherwise I'd get in trouble. Little ladies don't slam doors.)

This wasn't fair. This wasn't the way it was all supposed to work out. Cassandra Jovanovich was supposed to be my best friend. I knew it in my bones.

I tried to read a book – I'm halfway through *Little House on the Prairie* and Pa just brought home a cow and was trying to milk her – but I couldn't concentrate. I know things are really bad when I can't concentrate on a book. So I went to the kitchen and made a peanut-butter-and-banana sandwich. And out of the kitchen window, I saw Cassandra open her front door and let Kathy in. Kathy was wearing a John Lennon hat and go-go boots!

The peanut butter and banana stuck in my throat.

This was terrible. This was worse than terrible. This was a calamity. (A *calamity* is "a disaster accompanied by extensive evils.") If Kathy and Cassandra became best friends, I would have to run away from home. I knew that in my bones, too. I couldn't stand to see them together every day.

So I got my book and sat in the kitchen where I could keep watch on Cassandra's house. I mean, I didn't want to see them every day, but I had to know what was going on. And sure enough, in about ten minutes, they came out and turned the way to Kathy's house.

Cassandra would see the beer mugs. She'd probably tell Kathy I had told her about them. They'd laugh at me and Kathy would tell her why I was stupid. Why we weren't friends anymore.

This book is going ALL the WRONG way! I don't want to write about you-know-who, and now she's ALL I'm writing about.

I forced myself to read. I forced myself to read for one whole hour.

And then, I saw her. Cassandra Jovanovich. She came marching down the street and up her steps and into her house and slammed the front door!

I ran out into the backyard and up onto my tree branch so I could see into the Fergus kitchen. And I could see Mrs. Fergus saying something to Cassandra and she had her hands on her hips and was pointing at the front door. Then I saw Cassandra stamp her foot and shake her head. Then Mrs. Fergus said something else (Why, oh why, wasn't their kitchen window open?!?) and finally I saw Cassandra turn and leave the kitchen. So I scrambled down the tree, ran across the yard and back inside my house. And from the kitchen I saw her open her front door and close it slowly and quietly. Then she sat down on the bottom step and scrunched herself up into a little ball.

She looked very sorrowful.

I wondered if I should go to her.

But maybe she'd yell at me again.

But maybe she had a fight with Kat . . . you-know-who.

Maybe I was just being nosy if I went over.

What would Anne Shirley do?

And then I knew. I knew I had to give it another try. This was just one more trial and tribulation for my soul to bear. I would live through it.

I didn't slam any doors or make any noise. I just tiptoed across the driveway and went and sat down beside her.

Chapter 11

I was afraid to say anything.

But she said, "Why?"

I knew it! Kathy had told her everything!

"She told you?! Did she tell you what happened that day?"

She looked at me like I had two heads.

"What are you talking about? I want to know why you said you wanted to be an orphan."

I wanted to tell her. I wanted tell her about all the book orphans who have wonderful adventures. Anne and Mary and Jane. But Cassandra didn't look like she was having a wonderful time just this minute.

But then it came to me. "If you're an orphan, you can be whoever you want to be. Nobody owns you."

"Well, for sure nobody owns me," Cassandra said. "So what?"

"So you can do what you want. Nobody tells you you're stupid or asks who you think you are or tells you you can't do something when you grow up."

Cassandra put her head down and talked from behind her hair. "Oh what do you know? People tell me that stuff all the time."

"But it doesn't mean anything. You don't have to listen."

"Of course I do. I'm a kid."

I didn't say anything. And Cassandra Jovanovich just sat there looking at her boots. Then she said, "But maybe you're right. I have to listen to them, I mean, I have to do what I'm told, but . . . I don't have to . . . accept what they say. It's like I do what they tell me to do, but on the inside . . . I don't care."

I remembered all the times my mother said I couldn't be a writer. I started crying.

"What? What did I say? Why are you crying?"

And I just cried some more.

"Do your parents tell you you're stupid?" Cassandra asked.

I was shocked! My mother would never use the word stupid. Ladies don't.

"Because people tell me I'm stupid all the time. They

think just because my mother . . . just because . . . I'm not owned . . . that they can say any nasty mean spiteful thing that pops into their stupid heads."

I pulled up my shirt and wiped my nose. "My mother says I'm silly when I talk about being a writer and she says I can't do some things and she says who do I think I am." And then I pretended I was my mother.

"*Sniff.* And just who do you think you are? *Sniff.*" And I said it in a voice like I was sucking a lemon.

Cassandra laughed and said, "*Sniff sniff.* Who farted?"

I was shocked again! "My mother said ladies don't say fart. It's inappropriate."

"Oh fart. Fart fart FART! So there!"

This time I laughed at the shock of it. And then I remembered something.

"Want to hear a joke? Debbie Walker's mom told me. There was a woman who had lots of children and one day she thought maybe she was having another baby. So she went to the doctor, but he said don't be silly, you're too old to have another baby. All you've got is a little gas, said the doctor. So the woman went home but a few weeks later she went back to the doctor and said maybe she was getting ready to have another baby. The doctor said the same thing. Don't be silly. You're too old to have another baby. It's just a little gas. And then one day the woman went into the hospital and had twins! And then one day she was walking the twins in the baby buggy and she saw the doctor and he said what have we here? And she said oh nothing doctor. Just a couple of farts with bonnets on."

Cassandra and I laughed until we both had to run inside to the bathroom.

"So you get the joke?" I asked.

"Well, yeah. The doctor didn't know she was pregnant."

I looked at the floor.

"What?" Cassandra asked.

"My mother says not to say *pregnant*. Ladies say *expecting*."

Cassandra pushed her hair back and looked at me. "Do you know where babies come from?" she asked.

I know I blushed. "Of course. I mean . . . yes. I didn't before, but I do now. That's sort of what Kath . . ."

And when I was sitting on the toilet, Cassandra said, "Do you care what your mother says?"

"Well, yes . . . I mean . . ." I stopped talking and thought a bit. "Sometimes I just don't want to get in trouble. But sometimes I don't understand why she says what she says."

"So you think it's easier if you're an orphan?"

"Well, you can just make up your own mind about things. If you want to be a doctor or a singer or a movie star you can do it."

"What do you want to be?"

"I want to be a writer." I got up from the toilet and Cassandra took her turn.

"So? Do your parents hide the paper and pens?" she asked.

"No. But ..."

"But what? Tell you you're no good? So what? Do you have to listen to them?"

"If I say I want to be famous and special, they say I'm bragging. Why is it bragging?"

Cassandra didn't answer right away. She flushed the toilet and washed her hands, and then she said, "Maybe it's like the ugly duckling. You're really a swan and they don't know it and so they're trying real hard to keep you a duck like them."

I suddenly felt all warm because Cassandra had done it. She had used a story to explain something, like when I said Kathy is my Josie Pye. So she *was* a book person! Even if she didn't know it. I was sure now. She was going to be my kindred spirit! So now I wanted to be very considerate.

"But you're not like me. You can be what you want. No one is trying to keep you a duck."

"Yes, but how can I be an actress if I don't stay anywhere long enough to take drama lessons? I can't even be in a school play because I keep changing schools."

Cassandra opened a bathroom drawer and we got out Mrs. Fergus's pinkberry meringue lipstick and put it on. Then Cassandra found the Maybelline eye pencil and we drew dark lines around our eyes and filled in our eyebrows and then we sprayed ourselves with Mrs. Fergus's perfume, Evening in Paris. I don't know what I looked like but Cassandra looked really good. She looked like a real actress.

I suddenly got an idea.

"Do you want to be an actress?"

"More than anything in the world."

"I've written a play. It's about a prince and a princess who fall in love, but an evil witch separates them and then the flower fairy gets them together again. We can put it on in the backyard. We can sell tickets and everything."

For the first time Cassandra looked happy. She pushed back her hair and smiled. I told her she could be the beautiful princess. I thought she'd like that.

But Cassandra Jovanovich said she wanted to be the evil witch.

Chapter 12

We hurried over to my house and I got out my play.
Cassandra read it and I tried to read it over her shoulder.

"Well? Well? What do you think?"

"Sh!" But then she said, "Go away till I'm finished."

So I went and got *Little House on the Prairie* and I tried
to pay attention to Mary and Laura finding all the beads,
but for the second time in my life I couldn't concentrate.
My thoughts kept going to Cassandra Jovanovich. What if
she hated my play? That would be tragical!

Finally she looked up.

"It's pretty good."

I felt all electric inside. Then I tried again to convince
her to be the princess.

"SILENCE! How DARE you question ME you stupid TOAD?! I'LL teach you to open your mouth in MY presence! I'LL cut you up into little pieces and eat YOU for SUPPER!"

I stared at Cassandra.

"See? I'd be a great evil witch," she said.

I thought about her yelling like that at Paula or Susan or Debbie Oldman and I agreed she could be the evil witch.

"Why don't you be the beautiful princess?" she asked.

I remembered the time Mr. Morgan suddenly decided that we all had to recite a poem in front of the whole class instead of just to him privately and how I got hot and sweaty and heard this buzzing in my ears and how I forgot the very first line and everyone just stared at me.

"Oh, I couldn't. I . . . I just like writing."

"Then you're the director. You have to tell everybody what to do."

I liked that.

So we went outside to my trees in the backyard, and we talked about what to do next. Cassandra knew a lot.

"First we figure out who gets to be in the play."

So we went calling on other kids to ask them to join the play. Linda said she'd be the handsome prince, but only if Nancy was the beautiful princess. We said that was okay because Nancy is very pretty and has long black hair just like Snow White, and Linda is tall and thin with hardly any hair at all. Nancy said okay, too, but she wasn't going to play doctor if Linda tried that again.

By the time we got to Paula she'd heard about our play from Linda already and said she didn't want to be in our stupid play if she couldn't be the beautiful princess. How presumptuous!

Cassandra smiled at her.

"But we want you to be the witch's pet toad. You'd be just right."

Paula shrieked. "Do you know who I am, you stupid orphan? I can have you killed!"

"I know all about you, Paula. And I'm going to pay Ronnie and Donnie a whole dollar to beat you up once and for all!"

Paula ran away.

Cassandra laughed. "Let's ask Ronnie and Donnie to be my pet spider and toad. I bet they'd like that. Then they'd be our friends."

On the way to their house, we saw Laura Butterfield. She was sitting outside by herself and I showed her Cassandra Jovanovich.

Cassandra sat down. She pushed her hair out of her eyes and smiled at Laura.

"I want you to be in our play. I want you to be the

beautiful flower fairy who helps the beautiful princess," Cassandra told her.

I'd never thought of this. But now I looked at Laura and knew this was just right. Very appropriate. She was tiny and pale with long skinny arms and legs and lots of long blond hair that was almost white. She looked just like a fairy in a picture book.

Laura smiled and I could see where the new tooth was growing in. We asked her to come with us.

We all went to Debbie Walker's house and she said she'd be the beautiful princess's best friend and she said her dog, Tinkerbell, should be the fire-breathing dragon in one scene and the magic horse at the end.

Then we all went to Ronnie and Donnie's house. I couldn't believe Cassandra was doing this, but she did. She went right up to the door and banged. Both of them came outside.

"Paula wants you to beat me up, but I want you to be in our play. I'm going to be the evil witch and I need a toad and a spider."

Ronnie and Donnie didn't say anything. They just stood staring at Cassandra, which wasn't very considerate or appropriate, considering Cassandra was new.

And then Laura Butterfield stepped forward.

"Please," she whispered. And she looked so fairy-like

that I could tell Cassandra had picked the right person. And just like that, Ronnie and Donnie agreed to be in the play.

Everyone said they'd come to my backyard as soon as they told their moms.

And on the way home, I remembered something.

"What happened at Kathy's? I mean, I saw her call on you this morning. So I know you went out with her. But then you came home. Did you . . ." (*Oh, hope against hope!*) "Did you have a fight?"

"I don't like her," said Cassandra Jovanovich. (*Yes!*)

"She's bossy," said Cassandra. (*Yes!*)

"She wanted to play go-go dancers. She put on some music and we pretended to be go-go-dancers, but she wanted to be in front and she told me to stay behind her and just follow her. So I told her she was a dumb dancer."

(*Oh, be still my beating heart!*)

"Then she said I was a dumb orphan. So I left."

I knew I shouldn't feel happy that Kathy hurt Cassandra's feelings, but I couldn't help feeling a little bit of a thrill. But I said, "I'm sorry she said that. She's mean now. She didn't used to be. She was always bossy. She always told me I was wrong about everything. Like the time I told her Julie Andrews is my favorite actress, but she said *Mary Poppins* was a movie for babies."

Cassandra Jovanovich stopped walking and I banged into her. "I love *Mary Poppins*!" she said. "I've seen it three times!"

I knew it. I knew it in my heart of hearts Cassandra was destined to be my kindred spirit!

"I saw the beer mugs. You were right. They're ewww."

And then we were at my backyard.

Chapter 13

We worked on the play all week. But on Sunday, I had to go to church.

We go to church every Sunday. I have a bath every Saturday night to make sure I am clean enough. My mother says God doesn't like dirty little girls. I wonder if this means God doesn't like Paula. She goes to church, too, but a different one. I wonder if the God there minds that she smells.

I have to wear my best dress and my hat. Now that I am eleven, I don't have to wear the hat with the elastic that pinches under my chin.

"I am too grown up for that hat," I told my mother. "It isn't appropriate."

My mother just sniffed.

I also have to wear my best shoes. They fit okay in September when we buy them, but they always hurt my toes by April. All of the pictures that my mother takes of me are taken outside on Sundays when I am clean and dressed up. She always says to smile and I do, but if there are daffodils in the picture then I know it's spring and my shoes are hurting and my smile is fake. By July I have to walk on the backs of my shoes until September.

We drive to church every Sunday and we always leave at 10:15 sharp so my father can find a parking spot and not say bad words. When my father says bad words my mother glares at him but I bet she doesn't wallop his beee-hind.

I have to sit with my parents in our pew for the first few minutes of the service. Then the minister calls the children to the front and lets us all go to Sunday School. I like Sunday School. I didn't before, but that was before Mrs. McMillan became our new teacher. I think Mrs. McMillan is just like Anne Shirley's Mrs. Allan. She's pretty and sweet and she explains lots of things to us and always has cookies and juice.

"She makes the Bible fun," I told my mother. "Mrs. McMillan says the Bible is all about real people and real stories, just told in the funny way of talking they had back then."

Sniff. "Mrs. McMillan shouldn't say such nonsense," my mother scolds.

Usually we stay in the Sunday School room the whole time, but sometimes we come back into the Sanctuary when babies are getting baptized. Then we sing the baptismal hymn and we all look at this girl in our class named Sharon when we get to the line about Sharon's dewy nose and we wipe at our noses. But Mrs. McMillan told us it's really Sharon's dewy *rose* and means the plant called the Rose of Sharon. I like it that Mrs. McMillan explained this, but baptisms aren't as fun anymore, now that we can't tease Sharon. Well, it's still fun if the baby cries lots when the minister drops the water on its head.

I wondered about all of this water stuff so I looked up *baptism* in the dictionary. It means "to immerse in water." Some churches make you get right into the water, but not as a baby. When you're older. Not everybody wants to go for a swim in church so our church just puts drops of water on your head. I like this better because I wouldn't want strangers seeing me in my bathing suit. And besides, it seems inappropriate to be almost bare-naked in church. Mrs. McMillan explained that the drops of water were a symbol of getting right in the water and that getting right in the water was a symbol that you were being cleansed or purified. Without soap. Mrs. McMillan said it was a rebirth.

But *rebirth* doesn't mean coming out of your mother's tummy again. I think it means your personality changes. Maybe you become a better person.

"I can think of lots of people who should be reborn," I said to Mrs. McMillan. But she said that was inappropriate of me. I was getting tired of finding out I was inappropriate.

So baptisms are fun and as soon as they're over we get to go back to Sunday School. Usually there's a tea after church and the new parents bring in lots of cake and cookies.

One day when all of us were eating second and third helpings of everything, I heard the new mother say to Mrs. Kirkstone that her child would certainly never be a little pig like all of us. Ha! How presumptuous of her! Just wait until her little Elizabeth Victoria Margaret is our age and has to sit through sermons without moving. It makes you ravenous, let me tell you! (I looked up *ravenous* and it means the same as *rapacious*, which means that you are "accustomed to plundering," which means "seizing violent possession of something that isn't yours." Sometimes the boys plunder the cookies at these teas, so maybe the new mother is right.)

Sometimes we have a special church service. The thing I hate most about a special church service is we have to sit in our pews for the whole time. We don't get to leave and go to Sunday School with Mrs. McMillan. I have to sit very still for the whole hour and twenty minutes or my mother jabs her elbow into me. I have learned how to sit very still. I make up stories while the minister is talking. Once I made up a story that I was Lot's wife, turned to stone and unable to move, just like in the Bible. I did such a good job that I fell asleep and my mother jabbed me to wake me up. I had to go to my room when I got home. I don't think this was fair because I was thinking about the Bible the whole time.

Our pew is almost at the back of the church. I don't know why ours is at the back, but we have to sit there every Sunday or someone might glare at us. We all have to sit in our own pews. Once a new family sat down in Mrs. Kirkstone's pew. Mrs. Kirkstone stood there staring at this family until they figured out they had done something wrong and squeezed over. The next Sunday they sat behind Mrs. Kirkstone and they were stared at by the fox's eyes in the fox stole Mrs. Kirkstone wears around her neck. I think she arranged the fox head on purpose to make sure the eyes were on the new family. The Sunday after that, they moved to the other side of the church where the fox couldn't see them.

On the Sunday after Cassandra moved in, I told Mrs. McMillan all about how Anne of Green Gables liked going to Sunday School just like I do now with Mrs. McMillan to teach us. Mrs. McMillan said she had a surprise for me. After church was let out, she led me up to the Sanctuary part. Everyone was outside talking and we were alone. She showed me the glass case at the back. I had seen it lots of times but I never looked at it much because it was full of old papers. Mrs. McMillan showed me a letter. It was old and it was signed L.M. Montgomery. What was this?!

Mrs. McMillan told me that years ago, L.M. Montgomery's husband, who was a minister, spent a couple of weeks at our church in the summer when the regular minister was on holiday. She told me that L.M. Montgomery sat right there – and she pointed right there – for two Sundays in the pew saved for the minister's family.

I couldn't believe this. L.M. Montgomery in my church! I got all shivery, but this time I knew why.

I walked over to the minister's pew and sat down. I pretended I was L.M. Montgomery. I looked around me and pretended I was a famous author. I wondered what she had thought about. I wondered if she had paid attention to every word her husband said. But then I remembered that Anne Shirley liked to look out the window at the beautiful trees and flowers when the minister was talking, so I figured L.M. Montgomery was a lot like me and could make herself sit still by making up stories in her head.

I wondered if I sat there long enough, would I make up

stories like her? Then I realized that my bum was sitting right where L.M. Montgomery's bum had been. I wondered if she thought the pew was as hard as I did.

I wanted to tell Cassandra Jovanovich all about all this. So as soon as I got home, I ran next door.

"Cassie can't play with you today, Lee," said Mrs. Fergus.

"Why not? Where is she? Did she go to Kath –"

"Not that it is any of your business, Miss Mets, but Cassie has been sent to her room. She has behaved inappropriately."

Well! I knew all about that sort of thing!

So I went home. I helped my mother make supper (we always have a whole chicken for Sunday supper), and I waited and watched for Cassandra Jovanovich to come outside.

And when I saw Mr. and Mrs. Fergus drive away (they always play bridge on Sunday night), I snuck out.

Chapter 14

I didn't go to the front door. Somebody's mother would surely see me and tell. I went into my backyard and climbed over the fence and snuck up to Cassandra Jovanovich's bedroom window. It was open, but I didn't want to call out, so I threw a pebble at it.

Cassandra came right away. "Go away," she whispered.

"Why? What happened?"

"Go away."

I didn't want to go away. "Come outside. Mr. and Mrs. Fergus will be gone a long time. They always are. My mother says it's not right they're out so late on a Sunday, so I know."

Cassandra didn't answer me for a long time.

"Cassandra?" I called, but not loud.

Then I heard the side door open.

"If I'm caught . . ." she shook her head. "I'd better go back in." She turned to go, but I could see she looked really scared.

"What happened?" I asked again. "Did she spank you?"

Cassandra suddenly looked really mad. "I wish she had!" she said. And she spat it out like she did with her mother's name. "I wish she'd hit me. Then I would have hit her back! I would have hit her and hit her and . . ."

I know I just stared at her.

"I have to go back inside," she said.

But I grabbed her hand. "Don't go. I want to show you something." She looked back at the door, but she came with me.

We climbed over the fence into my backyard, then we snuck through the shadows to the far corner.

"This is my very special place," I told her. "No one knows about it." And I pulled her in under the bushes. My Sanctuary isn't very big, but I thought the two of us could scrunch in together if we huddled close. I lay down on the old leaves and Cassandra tried to sit.

"You have to lie down. It's important," I told her.

Cassandra made an angry noise, but she rolled over to her side.

"On your back. So you can look up," I said.

She rolled over.

"See? Look at all the stars. I call it my star window. And no one can see us. Nobody ever knows I'm here. I can just look up at the stars and think." And I told her all about the word *sanctuary* and about being home free.

Cassandra didn't say anything, and I was afraid to ask a question. So I watched the stars and I listened to the sounds of bugs and I could smell the damp earth and the dead leaves and the mint from Mrs. Carol's garden and the perfume from the roses. And it happened again, just like always. I felt shivery and happy and safe.

Then I told Cassandra all about L.M. Montgomery in my church. I thought she'd be thrilled for me. I waited for her to say so.

"She called my mother names," said Cassandra. "She said she was a terrible girl and . . . and . . . lots of other things, and she said I'd probably grow up just like her and . . ."

I pushed myself up. "Mrs. Fergus? Why? Why would she say such things? Your mother is dead. That's terrible."

"You don't understand. You don't understand anything."

And I could hear the hate in her voice. But I didn't think the hate was for me.

"Tell me. Please tell me. Then I can understand."

Cassandra turned away from me. "I can't. I'm not allowed."

I didn't understand any of this. So I tried to figure it out. "Did your mother and father do something awful? Is that how they died? Was it their fault? Or . . . or did they have a big fight with everyone just before they died? Is that it? And no one will forgive them?"

Nothing.

"Or maybe it was just fever, like Anne Shirley's parents. And maybe your family thought it was disgraceful and so they –"

"Shut up!"

"But why can't you talk about it? Why can't you talk about your parents? Don't you miss them? Didn't you love them?"

"No!" Cassandra spit.

So I said nothing.

"I didn't do my chores the right way for good old Cousin Doris. So she told me off, and I talked back. Then she said some really nice things about me and about my mom."

"And about your dad?" I prodded.

Silence.

And then, "And so I yelled back and got sent to my room. And that's all I want to tell you." And she lay back down on the dead leaves.

"But –"

"Shut up."

"But –"

"I said shut up!"

So I shut up.

"I know," Cassandra said. "Let's talk about you."

"Me?"

"Yeah. Let's talk about your little secret with Kathy."

So this was it. We would exchange secrets. I'd tell her mine and she'd tell me hers. Fine.

But not in here. Not in my Sanctuary. I didn't want to sully it. (*Sully* means "to destroy the purity of something.")

I got up and pushed aside the branches and leaves. Cassandra followed me and we went back to her yard.

"This is what happened," I said.

Chapter 15

As everybody knows, Kathy and I have been best friends or arch enemies since grade two. We had fights every day, but we always made up.

But not the last time.

Whenever we had money or could earn some money, like taking somebody's baby for a walk around the block, Kathy and I would run to Sid's Variety Store and buy candy, Popsicles, and chocolate bars, usually.

So one day I found three pop bottles in the park. That was six cents! I could buy us a Popsicle. Kathy didn't come with me because she had curlers in her hair. So I ran to Sid's and went up to the counter with my three pop bottles.

Someone had been there before me and left a case of

bottles on the counter. Six more bottles. Twelve more cents. I could buy us each a Popsicle and some licorice too! No one was at the counter and when Sid came out from the back, he said, "What do I owe you?" I don't know why. I don't. But it was an irresistible temptation. I pointed at all the bottles and said, "For nine pop bottles." And he just looked at me and didn't say anything. Then he said, "I don't think so." I know I went red as red can be and I knew he'd phone the police and I'd go to jail. So I turned and ran away. I left my pop bottles on the counter and ran out the door.

"I didn't want to tell Kathy when I got back, but she wanted to know where the Popsicle was and she got mad at me and said I was a pig and probably ate it all by myself so I told her and she promised not to tell."

"That's it?" asked Cassandra. "You tried to steal twelve cents?"

I nodded.

"That's the big drama in your life? Twelve cents?"

"I'm a thief," I said.

"You tried to be a thief, but you weren't any good at it."

"But I couldn't go back to Sid's ever again," I pointed out. "And I can't tell anybody why not."

"So Kathy told on you? Is that it?"

"No, she didn't. At least, not that I know about. But that's not it. You see . . ." and I got all red. Good thing it was dark.

"Kathy didn't stop going to Sid's Variety Store like me. And I knew why. She'd walk in and smile at Sid and he'd smile at her and then if there was no one else around, he'd show her pictures of bare-naked ladies in a magazine. And I said that wasn't right. I said my mother said being bare-naked was wrong and bad. And that's why she got so mad when we played doctor with Linda and showed our bums."

"So you told on Kathy?" asked Cassandra Jovanovich.

I shook my head. "No. Because she said being a thief was worse and she'd tell on me if I said anything. So then we didn't play much anymore. And then she was just . . . different. She stopped hanging around with us and went to Sid's almost every day after school."

"Oh, boy."

"Then she started picking on me all the time. She was mean every day and said mean things. And if she was playing with someone, she wouldn't let me play. And then . . ." I looked at Cassandra. "Do you know where babies come from?" I asked.

"Yeah," said Cassandra. "I know a lot about where babies come from."

I took a deep breath. "Well, I didn't. Not then. And Kathy knew that, and she made fun of me and said I was a big baby myself. And then this year all us kids went to see a movie at the school about making babies. Us girls went Tuesday night with our moms, and the boys went Wednesday night with their dads. And so now I know. So I'm not a baby, but Kathy won't stop saying mean things."

I finished talking and waited. Then Cassandra finally said, "She knows she's doing something wrong. She knows she shouldn't hang around Sid's. So she's mad at you for knowing about it. That's all it is."

I thought about this. It made sense. "So what do I do?"

"Just stay away from her. She's trouble," said Cassandra. "And she's going to get worse. Believe me."

"What do you mean?"

"Figure it out, Leanna. Some girls are like that. Loose, they call them. And just you wait. She'll get in trouble for sure."

I repeated "what do you mean" again.

"Girls like that get pregnant, okay?"

Pregnant!

"But she's eleven!" I said.

Cassandra hit me. "Not today, you idiot. But some day. Wanna bet?"

No, I didn't want to bet. I didn't want to think about Kathy in trouble. Right now, I just wanted to forget about her. And about me. And I knew how to do that.

So I said, "And now, you. What did Mrs. Fergus say about your parents?"

I waited for her to answer me. But she didn't say what I was expecting.

"Your initials are L.M., right?" she said. "You're practically L.M. Montgomery already. You just have to find a Montgomery to marry."

So she wasn't going to share her secret with me. Even after I told her my secret. This wasn't fair. But then right away, I understood. She wasn't mad at me. She just didn't want to talk yet. And she had given me a sort of present to make up for it.

L. M. Montgomery.

She was right! I had never thought of this! This was exciting. But then I couldn't think of anybody named Montgomery at school so the idea sort of fizzled out. I was in love with David, but his last name wasn't Montgomery.

"But you are halfway there," Cassandra Jovanovich pointed out. "Maybe you don't have to marry a Montgomery because then people would get confused at the library. But you could still go by L.M. something or other. And you have Anna in your name so it all fits together."

This is what Miss Gowdy calls having a brainstorm – sort of like the muse whispering in your ear.

Now I knew Cassandra Jovanovich was a kindred spirit. She just didn't know it herself!

Chapter 16

We worked hard all day Monday and figured we would be ready to put on our play on Tuesday. We finished up and I went inside for supper. But my mother was having one of her spells.

I always know when she's having one of her spells because she will be lying on the couch with a blanket over her, even her face. I think she's asleep, but I'm not sure, so I try not to make any noise. But today I was so excited about the play that I came running in and let the screen door slam with a bang. Then my mother sat right up and marched down to her bedroom. Then she slammed her door with a bang.

Well! Ladies aren't supposed to do that, but I didn't think I should say so.

I looked in the kitchen but there was no supper ready. I wondered if I should make something. I can make French toast and sloppy joes and s'mores because I learned at Brownies. But I knew my father didn't call this real food. So I was standing there, looking in the fridge when my father came home.

"Where's your mother?" he asked.

"She's lying down. She's having a spell," I said.

"*Humph*," said my father.

"Can you come to our play tomorrow?"

"What?"

I didn't tell him he should say pardon. I just reminded him about our play and then asked him again if he could come.

He shook his head. "Don't think so, kiddo."

I guess he saw the look on my face because then he said, "Tell you what. How about you and I go out tonight and get some grub? We'll celebrate the success of your play ahead of time."

This was a surprise! And then I had a brainstorm.

"Can Cassandra Jovanovich come, too?" I asked.

My father looked a little surprised. But then he said, "Sure. Why not?"

This was wonderful! I'd never taken a friend out for dinner before!

So I ran over to Cassandra Jovanovich's and Mrs. Fergus said yes and then the two of us ran back to my house and were ready to go.

My father came out of his bedroom. He didn't look too happy and I was suddenly afraid my mother said we couldn't go. But he smiled when he saw us and said to hop in the jalopy. My father says things like grub and jalopy when he's trying to be extra nice. I don't know why.

We both sat in the backseat and pretended we were rich ladies and my father was the chauffeur. And my father even let us listen to CHUM on the radio! We never listen to CHUM when my mother is in the car. We always have to listen to CFRB and then there's hardly any music, just a lot of old people talking.

"Where are we going?" I asked.

"You're supposed to tell me where to drive," answered my father. "I'm the chauffeur, remember?"

Well! This was a surprise. So I said, knowing my father would say no, "How about the Dairy Queen?"

"Very well, madam," he said, and Cassandra and I laughed.

So we drove for about fifteen minutes and we listened to The Beatles and The Dave Clark Five and Herman's Hermits and Simon and Garfunkel and then we were there.

I thought we were only going to get a cone, the same as always, or maybe a vanilla cone with chocolate dip for extra special, but my father said we could have whatever we wanted. And we weren't even having any real dinner!

So we both got a deluxe banana split and my father said that sounded good and he got one too.

"This is scrumptious," I said. That's a word Anne Shirley uses.

We sat at a picnic table and I said, "Did your dad ever take you to the Dairy Queen?"

I knew it was very daring of me to sneak this in, but maybe she wouldn't get mad at me this time, asking questions about her parents.

"No," she said. "No, my dad never took me to the Dairy Queen."

"But –"

My father butted in. "Well then, this really is a special day. How about we get something for the road?"

What was going on here?

"You mean we can have more ice cream?"

"Why not?" said my father.

So Cassandra and I headed back into the shop and ordered two chocolate milkshakes, and when we came out my father was back in the car, and we were headed home.

But we weren't.

My father turned onto Dixon Road and headed west. And I knew!

I poked Cassandra Jovanovich in the ribs with my elbow and smiled. "Guess where we're going?" I said.

"Dunno."

"The airport!"

"So?"

"So? Are you kidding? Haven't you ever been to the airport before?" I was amazed that she had missed this treat.

We drove and drove and then my father pulled over on the side of the road by the farmer's field and we got out and put the blanket from the trunk on the hood of the car and climbed up and lay down. Lots of other cars were parked along the road beside us.

We could see clear across the airport to where the planes started, and by the time they got to us, they were in flight. I screamed and screamed as they roared just over our heads.

For a bit, Cassandra didn't say anything. But by the time the third plane flew over, she was screaming too. My father just shook his head and smiled at us. And when he pulled out a package of cigarettes, I knew the deal. He walked along the side of the road, puffing away, saying something to the other dads, sometimes offering a light or even a cigarette. And I wouldn't tell my mother. She hated him smoking. Just like Marilla hated Matthew smoking and said (Marilla, that is), "What else could you expect from a mere man?"

So I turned away and Cassandra and I finished our chocolate milkshakes and we screamed at the top of our lungs.

"Where do you think they're all going?" asked Cassandra.

"Everywhere. All over the world."

"I wish I was on one," said Cassandra Jovanovich.

And I suddenly knew I could sneak in another question. "Have you ever been on a plane? Like, with your parents?"

But a plane was coming toward us and Cassandra pretended she didn't hear me.

It roared overhead and then everything was silent. So silent we could hear the birds in the fields. And it seemed odd, the jet scream and our screams and then the birdsong.

But it was getting dark and my father said we had to go home.

When we got home, Cassandra started to walk away and then turned to my father in a rush and said thank you. "Thank you, Mr. Mets. That was ... was ... truly one of the best –" She didn't finish.

"It's okay, honey. And you're welcome," said my father.

Honey?

Cassandra went inside and my father looked at me.

"Don't be asking her questions all the time. Sometimes, people just can't answer them."

Then my father went inside and I waited a moment and then hurried to my Sanctuary. I stared up at the stars and wondered where all those planes were now.

Chapter 17

Tuesday!

In the morning I showed Cassandra Jovanovich how I put a rope between the two biggest poplar trees and hung the curtain over it. When we pulled it back, the grass in between the trees made a really super stage. Then we sold tickets for five cents and made lemonade to sell when the play was over. Everybody came with a costume, and then we all did our make-up together.

Paula came by and said she wasn't buying a stupid ticket to our stupid Halloween party and didn't we know Halloween was in October? Then she called us all stupid and said, "Just you wait." But I didn't know what we were waiting for because Ronnie and Donnie liked being in the play and I didn't think they'd beat us up ever again.

But we really didn't care about Paula anymore because we were all having fun. I was supposed to be the director, but Cassandra really did everything. She showed Ronnie and Donnie how to sound scary and she showed Linda and Nancy how to look like real royalty. And she frightened everybody because she was so mean when she did the evil witch. But she always smiled at Laura Butterfield and then I saw that Ronnie and Donnie were always smiling at Laura Butterfield, too. I tried to figure out what it was about Laura Butterfield. I stared at her lots and then I knew.

She looked fragile. She looked like you could snap her in half. With her tiny body and white hair, she looked like the light could shine right through her. She didn't look real. That's why she made such a good fairy. She looked just like the fairies Arthur Rackham draws.

And I tried to understand why Ronnie and Donnie were so different around her. I figured it out, too. I think they wanted to protect her from breaking. I think instead of wanting to fight *with* everybody all the time, Ronnie and Donnie finally wanted to fight *for* something. And I knew that Laura Butterfield needed fighting for. And when I figured all of this out, I felt shivery down my spine. I had a new idea for another play. It would be about King Arthur and the Knights of the Round Table. And the princess they had to protect would be just like Laura Butterfield.

Soon everybody was there. Lots of kids came and even some parents. My mother brought cookies for after, but she said she wasn't paying five cents to get into her own backyard.

So we started, and we were pretty good until Tinkerbell grabbed the curtain and trotted around the yard with it. Everyone started laughing, but Cassandra just made up some lines and told everybody to be quiet or she'd turn them into toads. Then she grabbed Tinkerbell and tied him up. Ronnie and Donnie put the curtain back up and we got through the rest of the play.

The audience clapped at the end and we took a bow. And then Cassandra told everybody to wait a minute and called my name. She made me go to the front and she told them all that I was the writer of this wonderful play and they clapped for me, too. I smiled and waved and looked for my mother, but I guess she'd gone back inside.

Then we sat around and talked about how good we were and finished the lemonade and cookies. Then I got the cast to autograph my copy of the play because that's what they do in real theater and some day we might all be famous.

Then Ronnie and Donnie's mother said I had real talent and hoped I'd keep writing. And Debbie Walker's mother, Muriel, said I should write for Hollywood!

And when everyone else was gone, just Cassandra and I were left to clean up.

"We're a good team," Cassandra Jovanovich said. I felt a thrill!

"See?" I exclaimed. "We're kindred spirits. I knew it!"

Cassandra rolled her eyes, but she smiled at me. "You're an idiot! I just meant we're a good team. We should do this again – you write another play, and we'll put it on. Okay?"

"It'll be like Anne Shirley's story club. She and her friends . . ." I trailed off when I saw Cassandra Jovanovich's look. I made myself stop smiling. I made myself look stern. "Okay," I said. But on the inside I was jumping for joy.

I told my father all about the play at suppertime.

"It's too bad I missed it," he said.

Sniff. "You didn't miss much," my mother said.

"What do you mean?" I said. "We were wonderful. Everybody clapped."

"Don't talk back, Lee. And don't be silly."

"I'm not silly. You're silly!"

"Go to your room."

And I jumped up so hard my chair fell over behind me. I grabbed it and shoved it and I felt something crack open inside me and I screamed. I ran to my room and slammed the door and kicked it and kicked it over and over.

Nobody came after me. I could hear my parents fighting

in the kitchen. They yelled and said bad words and I could hear they were fighting about me and about lots of things all jumbled up together. Then I heard my mother go out and start the car and drive away. And I heard my father go downstairs to the basement.

I waited until it was dark and when I still didn't hear anything I opened my door and tiptoed down the hall. I snuck outside and hurried across the yard and into my Sanctuary.

I didn't want to be in the house. I wanted to be outside breathing in the night air. Night air never suffocates you. It's always fresh and smells like . . . it smells like life.

I stared at the stars and remembered the ugly duckling.

Chapter 18

I think this is the hardest part of my story. I thought about not writing it, about embellishing around it, but everybody knows anyway, so leaving it out would be stupid. Miss Gowdy says it's best to be straightforward when you have something difficult to say, so here goes.

I fell asleep outside in my Sanctuary and Cassandra Jovanovich found me in the middle of the night. She woke me up and then she told me.

I could tell she'd been crying. "What is it? What's wrong?"

"Oh Leanna. I'm so sorry. I'm so sorry."

And I was scared. "What? What happened? Did she hit you?"

Cassandra just shook her head. Then she grabbed for my hand. "You have to come. You have to come inside. Your mother – "

My mother? Was that it? My mother was mad at me? I suddenly realized how late it must be. I looked up and saw the moon had passed right over my sky window.

"I'm in trouble, aren't I?" I sat up.

Cassandra shook her head. "Leanna. It's your dad. It . . . he's . . . I'm so sorry. Your dad is . . . he died. And your mother found him and couldn't find you and phoned us and Doris woke me up and I knew where you were, or I thought I did, so I came out here and . . . and . . ."

My father was dead.

There.

Sometimes in books people say time stood still and I thought I knew what they meant, but I didn't back then. Now I do. It was as if the world stopped. As if everything was frozen and silent. Just one split second. And now everything was different. It was like someone had broken apart a block of ice. One half was before and one half was after and in between was this silent frozen air. Just for a second. Then it was gone.

If I have to write about this, then I want to be very honest about what I felt. I didn't cry. I could embellish this part and tell you I cried hysterically and beat my breast, but I didn't. I don't want to lie about my father's death. I believed Cassandra, but I didn't cry. What I felt was sick. This was my fault. I yelled at my parents. I made fun of my mother. I said I wanted to be an orphan and God heard me.

I followed Cassandra into the house. Mr. and Mrs. Fergus and Mrs. Petovsky were with my mother. She was crying and I just stood in the doorway looking at her.

"Leanna," she said and the sound came out all chokey. And I ran to her and hugged her and said I was sorry. She held me so tight it hurt, and I didn't mind. The hurting from hugging was better than the hurting that was going on inside.

Then our doctor came up from the basement and looked at us.

"I'm very sorry, Mrs. Mets. I think it was a heart attack. He probably died instantly."

Mrs. Petovsky helped my mother sit down.

Then everyone was talking and crying, but it was all just a loud buzzing in my head.

I wanted to see my father. I tried to get down the basement stairs, but Mr. Fergus held me back.

But then some men came and Mr. Fergus took them downstairs and they got my father outside and into a big black car.

"I want to see him," I said to one of the men.

"Now honey, you just wait. It isn't decent to see your father now. You'll see him sure enough later."

Then Mrs. Fergus said I could come home with them and eat breakfast over there. And I suddenly realized it was almost morning. My mother said run along because she had lots of phone calls to make.

Cassandra and I watched something on television, but I couldn't pay attention. When I realized that I was half an orphan I told Cassandra Jovanovich.

"I'm almost like you," I said. "I'm almost an orphan. Can someone be a half-orphan?"

Cassandra pushed back her hair and looked at me.

"Listen, Leanna," she began. But she stopped. "Never mind. I'm just ... really ... sorry about your dad."

In the afternoon my mom said to come home and have a bath – even though it wasn't Saturday night – before we went to the funeral parlor. And then our minister came and drove us. And when we got there, some of our relatives were waiting and then we got to go into the parlor first, before anybody else.

I'd never seen a dead person before. My father was lying there in his suit for church and his hands were folded on his chest. They were all clean and usually they never are because he always works in the garden. And his face had make-up on to make him look "natural," the undertaker said, but it made him look silly. I grabbed a tissue from the box on the table and tried to wipe it off, but somebody stopped me.

So then I stood back and tried to figure this all out. Everyone whispered as if my dad was sleeping and everyone went up to look at him and then said the same things over and over to my mother.

I stood where I could see my father and I just stared and stared. I couldn't get the hang of it. I couldn't figure out that this was my father and wasn't my father at the same time. He was there and he wasn't there. It didn't make sense. I tried to think about not being in my body but it was like trying to understand about infinity. Infinity goes on and on forever and ever. But I can't get the hang of that, either. Whenever I think about infinity, I always come up against an ending somewhere. I can't imagine forever. That's how I felt about trying to imagine what it was like to be dead. You can't imagine nothing.

And then I remembered something. Once, when I was little, I watched my father in the garden. He was wearing his beige shorts and no top and was dividing up the peonies. So I put on a pair of beige shorts and I took off my top and walked over to Debbie Walker's house.

Mrs. Walker laughed and said "Bless you, child. What are you doing?" I didn't know what she meant.

"You're half naked, silly," said one of Debbie's brothers.

"I want to look like my dad."

Mrs. Walker laughed again. "You are one to beat the band."

I didn't know what that meant. Then she gave me a shirt, and when I went home for supper, my mom asked where did I get that shirt and so I told her. But she didn't laugh. My dad did though. He laughed until tears came. And right now, looking at my dad's body, and remembering him laughing, I started to laugh, too.

Then Aunt Ethel grabbed me and told me to hush. "It's not seemly," she hissed. Then I laughed even harder. "I know," I told her. "I'm very inappropriate," and laughed even more. Aunt Ethel hauled me outside.

We stayed at the funeral parlor until late, and we were there all the next day, too. But before we left, I went out to the garden and cut some peonies. My dad had taken care of those bushes for a long time, and I thought they'd look nicer around his casket than the big, showy bouquets did. That's what Anne Shirley did when Matthew died. She gave him the flowers he loved.

On Friday morning my dad's sister and brother came to our house and we all got in this big, black car called a hearse. I made sure I didn't sit beside Uncle Bill. I was wearing a black dress that was itchy and hot and I could smell that my armpits were stinky. This was starting to happen to me a lot if I got hot, and I didn't like it. So I hated this dress. My Aunt Ethel had taken me shopping to buy me something black for today. She said I might as well get wear out of it for the winter, so she bought me this wool thing. But I'm never going to wear it again.

We drove to our church and lots of people were there waiting for us. They all went inside first and then we got out of the hearse and lined up behind the casket. We followed it up the aisle and someone was singing and we went right up to the front pew. I guess when someone dies you're allowed to sit in someone else's pew because this one sure wasn't ours.

The minister talked about my dad and all the things he did around the church and said we'd all miss him. Then we sang lots of hymns and listened to verses from the Bible.

I kept wondering when God was going to let everybody know that this was all my fault.

Chapter 19

Men loaded up the casket again and we drove to the cemetery and we all stood around the hole in the ground that was waiting for us.

Then the minister said some more things, but all I heard was "ashes to ashes and dust to dust," and then there was this roaring in my ears and I couldn't see anything. It all went black and I was pretty sure God was making me die.

And then I was sitting on a bench under a tree, and Mrs. McMillan was there with her arm around me, using her handkerchief to put water on my forehead.

I had a terrible headache and I knew right away that God had done something to me. But I wasn't dead and at least I could see again.

"Feeling better, Leanna?"

I looked at Mrs. McMillan. She is so pretty. I mean, she's old, but she looks kind all the time. She looks like she almost always smiles. Her eyes are dark blue and they never look cold. I felt the tears start. She hugged me tighter.

"You fainted, Leanna," she said. And for a moment I perked up because I had never fainted before, and I knew just how Anne Shirley felt because she had never fainted before and had always wanted to and then she did when she fell off the roof.

But then I felt mortified. Had all these people seen me faint? Did they see my underwear?

"We got you over here by the fountain and I told your mom I'd take care of you."

I watched Mrs. McMillan dip her handkerchief in the fountain and wring it out and then she put it on my forehead. Then I saw my mom talking a little ways away. And I looked at Mrs. McMillan again and I said, "I think my dad died because of me. I have behaved inappropriately." I told her everything.

When I finished she didn't laugh at me or look angry. She took my hands and smiled.

"Leanna. No one knows why bad things happen. But I am sure that little girls aren't punished for having bad thoughts or saying bad things about their parents. Why, we'd all be in lots of trouble if that were true."

I thought about this. I knew it was sort of true because I'd heard lots of kids complain about their moms or dads at school and they were all still alive. Then I remembered.

"But I said I wanted to be an orphan."

Mrs. McMillan nodded. "Yes, you did, and I think that was wrong. And I think if you are earnest and concentrate, maybe you'll figure things out in a less drastic way."

I wasn't sure what she meant and I asked.

"Leanna. There must be a way for you to be a writer without wishing your parents dead."

"Cassandra Jovanovich said I should just write and not worry."

"That's one solution. But it might be hard for an eleven-year-old girl to just ignore her mother. I think you have to find a way to tell her how much writing means to you."

She hugged me and kissed the top of my head and wiped my forehead with the wet hanky again. And I suddenly remembered how the minister puts water on babies' foreheads and kisses them when they're baptized. Maybe I had just been baptized by Mrs. McMillan.

She left me sitting on the bench. I closed my eyes and said I was sorry. I didn't want my father to die, and I really didn't want my mother to die, either. I was hoping God would hear me, so I kept my eyes squeezed tight to find out if I was forgiven. But all I heard was a bird singing in the rosebush behind me. I could smell the roses as the bird stirred the flowers.

Later that night I thought that maybe I had been answered after all. Maybe a bird singing and the perfume from a rose was how God said things nowadays.

me. Maybe inside me. This isn't coming out right. What I mean is, I was afraid when I moved to our apartment my father wouldn't belong there. I'd start to forget about him. But here I was, way up north at the Fergus cottage and my father had never been here. He didn't belong here. But I felt like my father was as close to me as could be. I don't know why. Maybe I can ask Mrs. McMillan.

But without having to ask anybody, I was very sure that my father could see the moon that I could see and hear the loon that I could hear.

Chapter 23

Every day at the cottage was almost the same. We ate and swam and went fishing and learned how to dive off the diving rock. It was called the diving rock because the water was deep there and you wouldn't get hurt diving down. Cassandra and I tried to touch the bottom, but we never did. I'd stretch out my toes, but just when I thought maybe, *maybe* I'd touch, the water would push me back up. And every day, Mrs. Fergus gave us some chores to do. We had to pump water and heat it up and do the dishes and sweep the floor.

One day when it was raining, I wanted to start reading *Cue for Treason*. I couldn't believe I hadn't read one bit of one book yet, but Mrs. Fergus told us to clean up our bedroom. We got the broom and went way under our bed. I don't think anyone had cleaned under there for a long time. We pulled out piles and piles of dust, candy wrappers, a baby bottle, and a pair of someone's dirty underpants that were dirty both sides like they didn't have a change and had to wear them inside out.

We showed them to Mrs. Fergus and Mr. Fergus said, "Those are quite the racing stripes!"

Then Mrs. Fergus hit him and said, "Ray! Not in front of the you-know-who!" (By which she meant Cassandra and me.) Then Mr. Fergus pinched his nose and took the underpants from us and held them at arm's length and marched outside.

Cassandra and I finally figured out what racing stripes were and after we got over the ewie-ness of it, we laughed like a couple of hyenas.

That's what Mrs. Fergus said. "Really, girls. You sound like a couple of hyenas. Try to behave like young ladies!"

"You sound just like my mother," I told Mrs. Fergus.

Mrs. Fergus nodded. "Well, of course, Lee. In our day, we knew what was what."

"See? My mother says that all the time! What does *we knew what was what* mean?" I asked. "And what is *what*? I mean, *what* is what?" I just couldn't get my question to come out right.

"That's enough, Lee," said Mrs. Fergus.

We just laughed even more and went back to our room. We didn't want to find anything else after the underpants, I can tell you, but we did. On our next sweep, we pulled out a book. It was yellowed and the cover was crumpled and lots of page corners were folded down. Cassandra Jovanovich straightened out the cover and showed it to me.

It was what my mother calls dirty. And I don't mean from dust under the bed. It showed a lady with a dress that showed a lot of her chest and a man was touching her there and she was smiling. I was pretty sure my mother would find the strength to wallop my beee-hind if she could see me now.

And then, I suddenly thought of Kathy.

Cassandra and I looked at each other. And then Cassandra put a chair in front of our door and wiped the dust off of the book. I sat on the bed and Cassandra sat in the chair and read in a loud whisper.

The people said lots of stupid things to each other about love. But then Cassandra read a page where the corner was folded down. The man and lady were naked in a swimming pool and he kept talking about her breasts. Big buttery breasts, he said, and they bobbed up on top of the water. Then Mrs. Fergus knocked on our door and wanted to know what we were whispering about. Cassandra shoved the book under the mattress and said we were reading. It was the truth, but it was a lie, too.

By then the rain had stopped and we put on our bathing suits. Mrs. Fergus came down with us, but then said she was too hot to stay out and went up to lie down. But soon she came marching back waving something in the air. It was our book. She said that Mr. Fergus was sleeping in their bed so she went to lie down on our bed and found this. And when she said THIS, it was in capital letters, and she waved the book in the air.

"Well?" she demanded.

I was going to ask how she found it because it was shoved way under the mattress and it didn't even make a bump and I didn't think Mrs. Fergus was like the princess and the pea and could feel things under the mattress to prove she was fancy. So I think she was snooping on purpose. But before I could say anything, Cassandra said, "What is it?"

And Mrs. Fergus said, "I beg your pardon?" and sounded just like my mother when I know I'm going to get it.

Cassandra shoved her hair over her face and said again, "What is it?" and reached out to take the book. Mrs. Fergus snatched her arm back and held the book up and behind her head like she was going to swat a mosquito.

"Are you telling me you've never seen this book?" she asked.

"I can't even see it now," Cassandra answered.

Mrs. Fergus looked back and forth at both of us. Then she put her arm down behind her back.

"This is a piece of filth," she said. Then again, "FILTH!" in capital letters. "It's going in the fire." She marched off and Cassandra and I swam out to the raft.

"She snooped," I said.

"All adults snoop," said Cassandra. "They pretend they're doing it to help you, but they just want to catch you doing something wrong."

I thought about this and nodded. It had never occurred to me before that my mother snooped. But suddenly, I knew how she knew I loved David. She had looked in my underwear drawer and found the letter I wrote him, but never sent to him. And even though this happened way back last year, I felt suddenly angry as if it just happened now. I was planning out a better hiding place when I wondered about something else.

"Why is it filth?" I asked. "Lots of people touch each other and get married and have babies. Why does she say *FILTH* like that?"

"Because the people in this book aren't married."

And then I suddenly had a brainstorm. *So-called Mrs. Harris!* And I knew! The mothers always said "so-called *Mrs.* Harris." They meant she wasn't a "Mrs." They meant she wasn't married. I felt a wonderful sense of satisfaction. I had just solved one of those perplexing adult puzzles.

Cassandra was still talking. "Or maybe Doris is mad because Ray won't touch her like that and that's why they don't have any babies," she said.

And then we both thought about Mr. and Mrs. Fergus touching and saying dirty things like in the book and we laughed like a couple of hyenas until we hiccupped.

"I wonder what it would be like to have big buttery breasts?" Cassandra asked.

I looked down at my chest and I wondered too.

Chapter 24

The people at the cottage next door came over one night and asked us to join them later for a sauna. A sauna is what the wooden shack is that they have right down on the water. They heat it up really hot and sit in it and sweat. Then when they're so hot they can't stand it, they run outside and jump in the lake naked.

Mr. and Mrs. Pedersson were very nice. She made lots of desserts and called Cassandra and me over to eat them. Mrs. Fergus bought store-bought desserts because she said she was at the cottage and didn't want to work. But Mrs. Pedersson said it wasn't work to bake desserts, and so we got to eat all kinds of different things I'd never had before. I especially liked the little buns she made with cardamom seed. Mrs. Fergus said she never used cardamom seed and it must be something foreigners use.

One day they let us see inside their sauna. It was all wood and the wood was almost white and very shiny. There was a big bucket they filled with water and then poured it on the burner when the burner got very hot. They had something called a loofah that they used to rub their skin before they got all sweaty. They said it rubbed all the old skin off and then your skin was soft as a baby's bum. Everything smelled nice, like you were in the middle of a wet forest.

Mr. Pedersson said it was very healthy to take a sauna. He said it got poisons out of your body. He said it made you relax and then it made you sleep very deeply.

Mrs. Fergus said that was all hogwash. She said there were no poisons in her body and how she slept was her own business. But I liked listening to the Pederssons talk about the sauna. It reminded me of all the things I had learned in school in social studies about other lands and people. And when they showed us pictures of where they grew up, it was different from the pictures that were in our books at school. Maybe I will go to Sweden one day when I'm older.

There were only a couple of days of our week left when the Pederssons asked us over to the sauna. Mr. Fergus said maybe they would be over later, but Mrs. Fergus looked like a mouse had run up her leg and her mouth puckered up and she said "Certainly not." Then when the neighbors were gone, she yelled at Mr. Fergus and said he'd had too much beer and sitting around naked was disgusting.

"But they don't sit around naked," I told her. "Mr. Pedersson says they wrap themselves in towels while they sit in the sauna and then they drop them right when they go in the water. And it's at night so nobody sees you."

Mrs. Fergus looked at me like I was a bug. "I don't recall asking for your opinion, Miss Mets," she said. And her voice sounded all frozen.

It was a warning, I could tell, but Cassandra ignored it. "It sounds like fun being naked underwater," she said.

Mrs. Fergus banged a spoon down on the counter. "That's enough!" she said. "I'm sure with your background it would seem like fun. Any more of this talk and Lee will be sent home and you will be packed off now, instead of in two weeks. I won't have it, do you hear me?"

Cassandra's eyes were flashing, but she didn't say anything.

"Do you hear me?" Mrs. Fergus said again.

"Yes." She spit out the word.

"And furthermore, I don't want you girls spending any more time with those Pederssons. Is that clear?"

We both nodded.

Then Mrs. Fergus marched into her bedroom and

slammed the door. Cassandra started to cry and ran outside. I ran after her, but I didn't see where she had gone. I called her name but she didn't answer.

I went inside and Mr. Fergus was asleep on the couch, so I cleaned up the supper dishes. Cassandra Jovanovich came back, but she wouldn't talk to me. We went to bed still not talking and I lay there for a long time wide awake. I was pretty sure there were poisons in my body.

Chapter 25

It didn't rain at all the next two days and we spent every minute outside. Mrs. Fergus seemed to forget about yelling at all of us and just acted like the whole thing had never happened. She even made a cake from scratch. But I knew Cassandra hadn't forgotten.

"Whenever I do something someone doesn't like, they threaten to pack me off," she said. "See Leanna? That's what happens if you're not 'owned.' No one has to care about you long term. They just . . . just borrow you – like a book – for a while."

Cassandra had become all sulky and kept her hair over her face, so I couldn't get a good look at her, and I knew she was thinking about packing and leaving the cottage and then packing and leaving the Fergus's. I was pretty sure we wouldn't be having too much fun anymore.

And then before we knew it, it was the last day at the cottage. Cassandra was all jumpy and prickly, like a thunderstorm was coming. Well, it was more like Cassandra *was* a thunderstorm, just waiting to start. And after Mr. and Mrs. Fergus took the little boat and went to visit the Smiths up the lake for the evening, Cassandra let out all the thunder and lightning that was inside her.

This is what happened.

I started talking about *Anne of Green Gables* again and told her she had to read it.

"I know what I said about orphans and that it's not as fun as I thought, but you know Anne's my favorite book and you still haven't read it. And now that I'm half an orphan, I like Anne even more. So please, please, please – "

Cassandra Jovanovich jumped out of the chair and screamed, "You and your stupid orphans! I hate your stupid orphans! And I hate you for being so stupid!" She was crying and screaming and waving her arms up and down. "I'm not an orphan! Do you hear me? I'm not an orphan. I never was! I just pretend because my mother didn't . . . DOES not want me! *Present* tense. Everybody's embarrassed because I'm not wanted by my mother! She wasn't married and nobody knows who my father is. She wouldn't ever tell. Rita got pregnant when she was fifteen. *Fifteen*! And here I am. And nobody wants to talk about it. I'm not allowed to tell anyone. And she just ran away. Nobody knows where she is. Everybody takes me for a while and then passes me along. I don't belong to anybody! I'm not an orphan! I'm just not wanted! You don't want to be owned. Well I *am* owned and my owner doesn't want me!"

Then she ran out of the cottage. The back door slammed like a gunshot.

I just stood there. I couldn't take it in. And then everything just shifted in my head in an instant and it all made sense. Why she wouldn't talk to me, tell me her secret, anything about her parents. She must hate me.
And then suddenly, I was afraid for her. What was she going to do?

I was out the back door in a second. She was only just ahead of me. She ran up the hill and over the hydro-line clearing and down the other side of the hill. She stumbled and so did I, but we didn't stop running. I knew I was cut, but I kept following her because I was afraid. Then I tripped and slid down the hill and banged into her and knocked her down. She jumped up and looked all about, as if she hadn't seen the diving rock before. As if she was looking at it for the first time. All of a sudden she was flying across the ground and took a huge jump into the air. I followed a foot behind her, and we tumbled together into the lake.

We came up at the same time and I checked for my glasses with one hand and grabbed her shirt and hung on tight with the other. She was still crying and there was stuff from her nose on her lip, but I didn't let go.

She smacked at my arm in the water. "Get away from me. Go away!" she shouted.

"No! I don't care if you're not an orphan," I shouted back. "You're the best friend I ever had, and I don't care about anything else." This was true. I didn't have to think about it, even. The words just came out of my mouth and they were true.

Cassandra stopped pushing me. All the fight just collapsed out of her. I let go of her shirt and she swam back to the rock. I followed right behind her.

She sat down and let out a sigh that sounded like it came all the way up from her belly button.

"I am so sick of lying. To everybody. But mostly to you. Especially after your father died. I felt terrible. But I couldn't tell you the truth. But you see Leanna, it doesn't make me special that no one wants me. It just makes me nothing."

"You're not nothing," I said. I wanted to say more, but

I didn't have the words. I didn't know how to say what I felt like inside. It was just like the ache I felt when Miss Gowdy read to us. I had all this . . . desire inside and I didn't have the words. But I did know one thing, and I could tell Cassandra this.

"You are my friend. It's true. And not because you're an orphan, I mean because I *thought* you were an orphan. But because you're . . . you're . . . you. You're exciting. You make me think about things. I mean, really think." I thought about Laura Butterfield, and about how I suddenly saw her as so fragile. But Cassandra Jovanovich was the opposite. "You're so strong," I told her. "You just don't know it."

Cassandra looked at me.

"When we go home and I'm gone, will you still be my friend?" she asked.

"I promise," I told her. "I will write letters to you all the time. And I'm good at writing letters. I say things better when I write them. I have time to think about the right words."

Cassandra smiled at me. "I will miss you very much, Leanna. But I'm glad I'm leaving. I hate Doris and Ray and all their stupid rules."

Then she jumped up from the rocks. "Do you want to go skinny-dipping?"

"But Mrs. Fergus said no. We'll get in trouble."

Cassandra put her hand up to her eyes and pretended she was looking around.

"Nope. Can't see her. She's not here."

Then she looked behind a tree and behind the big rock. She was so silly, I laughed.

Then she pulled off her blouse and pulled down her shorts. "I don't care what Doris says anymore. She's passing me along now, so I don't care. And why can't we go skinny-dipping? Why is it *DISGUSTING*? Why is it *FILTH*?" And she said both words in capital letters and she sounded just like Mrs. Fergus.

I didn't know. I don't know why adults have so many rules.

So I took my off my blouse and shorts. And this time I remembered to take off my glasses. We stood there in our underpants.

Cassandra looked at me. "I dare you," she said.

And so I stuck my tongue out at Cassandra and pulled down my underpants first. Then she pulled down hers and I took her hand and yanked. We took three running steps and leaped into the water, holding hands. We went down, down, fast at first, then slower. And then, for the first time all week, I touched bottom. I stretched out my toes and touched! It was because of Cassandra. Cassandra and me together, we were heavy enough to sink to the bottom. And

I felt the rock and sand and dead leaves at the bottom of the lake. And then that funny feeling that you're getting lighter and lighter until the water can't hold you down anymore and spits you back up to the air and sky. We bobbed back to the surface, still holding hands.

We floated on our backs and looked at all the stars. You couldn't begin to count the stars, ever. It was just like being at home in my secret spot. It was just like I'd brought my Sanctuary along to the cottage with me. Except I didn't have a little star window to look up at. I was looking at all of the heavens. I was looking into infinity.

And suddenly it was like a lightning bolt had struck me. And I knew something really important. My Sanctuary wasn't like other sanctuaries, like the ones made out of wood and stone in churches. So it didn't matter if my mother and I moved. I wouldn't be leaving my Sanctuary behind. My Sanctuary was wherever I was. It would be with me always if I just looked up and looked inside myself.

We swam back to shore, and we climbed up the rock and lay down again. I stretched out my arms and legs as far as they could go, stretching my fingers and toes and reaching all over the rock. Then I rolled over and did the same thing lying on my stomach. I felt like I was part of the rock.

"This rock is a real pain in the ass," Cassandra said. And we knew she was saying a bad word, so we started to laugh.

Then Cassandra said *ass* again in a louder voice and then we both shouted *ass* several times into the dark.

"Of course, if we had buttery breasts to lie on, it probably wouldn't hurt at all," she said.

Then we were both laughing as hard as we had been crying before. I thought of what Mrs. Fergus would say if she heard us say *ass* and *buttery breasts* and I laughed harder still because here in the dark it was wicked and dangerous and wonderful all at the same time. Then I was laughing so hard that I couldn't help it and I started to pee right there on the rock.

I jumped in the water again to hide the pee and when I got out, I knew the words.

"It doesn't matter if you don't belong to someone if you know you belong to all this," I told Cassandra. "The rock and the water and the stars." I sat up and looked around. And then it happened. The muse came! "Ashes to ashes and dust to dust. That's what the minister said at the funeral. I think it means we go back to what we came from. So that must mean we came from the earth and we go back to the earth. So we belong to this. All this earth. So that must mean the earth owns us."

I held my arms out wide. "You see, you do belong to something, Cassandra. And so do I. And it's bigger than Doris and Marjorie and Rita. I don't need my Sanctuary in the backyard anymore because I think Sanctuary is everywhere. If we're part of all of this, then we can say 'Home Free!' wherever we are. Whenever we need to."

Cassandra didn't say anything. Then, after a long time, she reached for my hand. "Thank you," she whispered.

And I felt like I was big enough to hold all the rock and all the water and all the stars inside of me forever.

Chapter 26
(My Last Chapter)

I showed Miss Gowdy my story up to now, and Miss Gowdy says I should stop soon. She says my last chapter was just right and could be my last chapter because it had a strong ending. She says sometimes writers don't know when to stop and have to be reined in like horses. But I have to write just a bit more.

We left the next day for home, and Cassandra left two weeks later for the next relative. I helped her pack, and I cried a lot. But Cassandra didn't cry. She said she was happy to leave Doris and Ray and she would miss me very much, but she knew I'd send her letters. She had been packing without looking at me, but now she suddenly turned and faced me.

"Are you going to be a writer?" she asked.

I started to answer, but she went right on like my mother does when she asks me something but has no intention of letting me say anything.

"Because I'm going to be an actress. When I get to Mary and Peter's I am going to say I HAVE to have drama lessons. I loved being in your play. I want to be in lots of plays. I want to get up on the stage and have everybody look at me. I want everybody to see me."

And then Cassandra Jovanovich did a wonderful thing. She looked in the mirror and pulled all of her hair back into a ponytail high up on her head. Then she turned to look at me.

"From now on, people are going to see me. I want the world to see me."

I jumped up and hugged her.

"Thou art my bosom friend," I said, "and I love thee with all my heart."

Cassandra laughed. "Thou art crazy," she said. And then, wonder of wonders, she gave me her John Lennon hat!

Mary and Peter came that afternoon and I don't know how I said good-bye. I held on to Cassandra Jovanovich and didn't think I could ever let go. I couldn't believe I'd only known Cassandra for a few weeks. I couldn't remember what it was like before. So I stood there and hugged her and I wished something would happen, like an earthquake, so it wouldn't be me choosing to let go. Then my mother put her hand on my shoulder and smiled at Cassandra.

"Good luck, dear," she said.

And then my arms slipped down and my mother was holding me and I watched Cassandra get into the car and close the door. I watched her drive up the street and around the corner and I didn't move. Doris and Ray went inside and my mother and I stood in the driveway.

Then my mother led me inside and handed me a small package. I opened it and just stared. It was a copy of *Anne of Green Gables*.

"I don't understand," I said.

"It's yours," said my mother. "Your own copy to keep."

I think my mouth fell open. I didn't think I could ever be shocked like that. I was wrong, because when I went to thank my mother, she said, "Don't thank me. I found it in your father's drawer when I was sorting his clothes."

"Dad?"

She nodded. "Read the front page."

So I did, and it said "To Leanna. Keep your nose in a book. Love, Daddy."

"But . . . when was he going to give it to me?"

My mother shrugged. "He knew you liked it. I guess he

bought it and put it away and maybe forgot about it. Or maybe he was keeping it for something special."

He *knew* I liked it? How did he know that? He never talked to me about Anne Shirley. He never said anything except . . . you've always got your nose in a book.

Well! This was becoming a very upside down day. And then it got even more upside down. I was beginning to feel like Alice in Wonderland because my mom said, "I read it when I found it. I can see why you like it. That Marilla is quite the character."

I was speechless!

But the day wasn't over yet because then my mother said, "Maybe next summer, if we get enough money when I sell the house, we could go on a holiday. I've always wanted to go to Prince Edward Island. We could drive and stay at the seaside."

It was that time-stood-still thing again. One moment you were on one side of reality and the next you were on the other. Prince Edward Island! I could go to Green Gables! I could see the Lake of Shining Waters and Anne's bedroom and the Haunted Woods and –

My mother was saying something.

"What?"

"Pardon."

"What?"

My mother sighed. "Leanna. Young ladies say pardon."

"Pardon?"

"I was saying, we should go shopping soon. You're in grade six now. You'll need a brassiere."

Well!

I screamed and hugged my mother as hard as I could. And then I laughed because my mother sniffed and said, "My goodness, Lee, calm down!" But I couldn't calm down. I ran to my bedroom and wrote a letter to Cassandra.

I got a letter from Cassandra one week later and she said they are going to let her take drama lessons twice a week. One is a private lesson and one is a group play and she starts in September.

I didn't think I could be any happier, but then I got to be in the Writing Club. This is how it happened.

Just after school started, my mother and I were at church. It was one of those special services and I had to sit in our pew the whole time. And I hope I don't get in trouble for saying this, but I didn't listen to the minister at all. I thought about L.M. Montgomery and I thought about making up stories and I thought about my father and I wondered if I had really been forgiven.

And this time I didn't fall asleep. This time I made up a poem about my father. I wrote it down as soon as I got home so I wouldn't forget it. I showed it to Mrs. McMillan the next week at Sunday School and she showed it to our minister. When our minister came to talk to us about my father, he told my mother about my poem. I hadn't told her, so she was surprised. But then I was surprised because the minister pulled it out of his Bible and read it out loud.

Ode To My Father (Earl Mets)

When all the stars shine bright at night,
I know in my heart thou art gone.
But I remember your smile,
And I remember your laugh,
And I will never forget your song.

Then the minister said he wouldn't be surprised if I didn't become a writer when I grew up.

So, it was as simple as that. My mother let me be in the Writing Club as soon as it started. And then she said the most amazing thing! She said, "You have to follow your star, Leanna."

Author's Afterword

There is just one more thing. (Sorry Miss Gowdy.)

On the last day when we were at the cottage, I hunted around until I found the perfect rock. It wasn't too big and it was a piece of the Canadian Shield, the oldest rock in the world, and it had a nice hunk of quartz in it. I took the rock and dropped it from high up onto another rock and my rock broke in half, both pieces red and brown and sparkly with veins of quartz. I gave one half to Cassandra.

And in her letter, Cassandra said the rock sits on her desk and she touches it every night when she gets in bed and every morning when she wakes up and when she touches it she says "Home Free."

My half sat on my dresser until I got Cassandra's letter so then I moved it to my desk where I write my stories.

I touch it every morning and every night and I say "Home Free" too.

THE END

SHARON JENNINGS is an editor and award-winning author, having written over 60 books for young people. As a girl Sharon enjoyed writing plays, just like Lee. Although, unlike Lee, she always cast herself in the starring role. Sharon lives in Toronto.